Edward C. Lefroy, Wilfred A. Gill, John A. Symonds

Edward Cracroft Lefroy

his life and poems including a reprint of Echoes from Theocritus

Edward C. Lefroy, Wilfred A. Gill, John A. Symonds

Edward Cracroft Lefroy

his life and poems including a reprint of Echoes from Theocritus

ISBN/EAN: 9783337252373

Printed in Europe, USA, Canada, Australia, Japan

Cover: Foto ©Andreas Hilbeck / pixelio.de

More available books at **www.hansebooks.com**

Edward Cracroft Lefroy

His Life and Poems including a
Reprint of Echoes from Theocritus

By Wilfred Austin Gill

With a Critical Estimate
of the Sonnets by the late
John Addington Symonds

John Lane, *The Bodley Head*
London & New York   mdcccxcvii

PREFACE

This little book calls for a few lines of justification. In 1885 the Rev. Edward Cracroft Lefroy published a volume of one hundred Sonnets ("Echoes from Theocritus and other Sonnets," Elliot Stock) in which literary critics at once recognised the true ring of poetry. Lefroy died in 1891 at the age of thirty-six. Shortly after his death, the late Mr. John Addington Symonds lighted upon this volume in one of the batches of books which were periodically sent out to him from England to his winter home in the Engadine. He instinctively singled it out as the production of a genuine poet. In a correspondence which ensued he repeatedly expressed to me his desire that these Sonnets should not be allowed to die. The book is now out of print, and Symonds's high estimate of Lefroy's work, even were it not endorsed by that of other competent authorities, would seem to furnish sufficient ground for the reprinting of the Sonnets.

But the personal side of Lefroy is seen only indistinctly through his poems. When I had told him something of the man and his conversation, Symonds intuitively perceived that "his life philosophy was even more noteworthy than his verse." In order, therefore, to bring the *complete* personality of Lefroy into clearer light, I gladly acceded to Symonds's suggestion that we should write a joint-memoir, he supplying a critical appreciation of the poems, and I contributing the personal side which friendship from boyhood had rendered familiar to me.

The execution of our design was unfortunately frustrated by Symonds's death. He wrote, however, what he called a "first effort," which appeared in the *New Review* of March 1892, and subsequently, with some additions, in "In the Key of Blue." By the kind permission of Mr. Elkin Mathews, the publisher, and of Mr. Horatio Brown, Symonds's literary executor, this essay is now substantially reproduced in the appendix.

The estimate, even as it stands, is a valuable testimony to Lefroy's genius, but one must deeply regret that Symonds did not live to bring out in fuller detail his general sympathy—in spite of some vital points of divergence—with Lefroy's religious, Hellenic, and poetical temperament.

Left to complete the memoir alone, I have attempted to pay a simple tribute of affection to a gifted friend, from whom I have learned much, and others may care to learn something.

One word of warning. Those who hold that a biography, to be of any interest, must be either a record of striking personal doings, or a mine of epistolary gossip between men of mark, will find little to detain them in this volume.

It mainly consists of suggestions offered by a man of candid and cultivated mind upon many subjects of general interest—not least in the present day—subjects which most men have not the patience to think out, or in some cases the courage to face. The peculiar merit of Lefroy's opinions lies, I think, in their being at once liberal and definite.

An apology is due to the personal friends of Lefroy for the delay—owing to pressure of other work—in the publication of this memoir. But since it contains little that concerns current events, I believe that such interest as the book may possess will not be affected by the lateness of its appearance.

A selection from Lefroy's Lyrical poems now appears for the first time in a collected form. In Chapter III. (pp. 46, 47) I have stated his reasons for neglecting this kind of versification. Many of his Lyrics were left in the rough, and it would therefore be unfair to judge him by these, but they deserve a place among his literary remains if only to illustrate other sides of his temperament.

Of the thirty new Sonnets now printed, some have already appeared in a fugitive form: some of the rest derive an interest from the date of their composition— the year of his death.

I have given the names of Lefroy's correspondents only in the case of letters addressed *to* him. Where the letters are written *by* him, their importance depends but slightly, if at all, upon the personality of the recipient.

The headings to each chapter and the quotation which closes the memoir are taken from Lefroy's diaries. They are very characteristic of the man.

I have to thank several of Lefroy's friends for the loan of his letters, especially Mr. Edward C. Price, to whom I am also indebted for looking over the MS. of the memoir and making some suggestions which I have gladly adopted.

W. A. G.

MAGDALENE COLLEGE, CAMBRIDGE,
Oct. 28, 1896.

CONTENTS

MISCELLANEOUS SONNETS:

PAGE

THIRTY SONNETS NOT INCLUDED IN THE 1885 VOLUME:

CONTENTS

LYRICAL POEMS:

CONTENTS

MEMOIR

CHAPTER I

Not to be first : how hard to learn
That lifelong lesson of the past ;
Line graven on line, and stroke on stroke ;
But, thank God, learned at last.
                                    CHRISTINA ROSSETTI.

EVEN in memoirs of eminent men, it is rarely necessary
to dwell at length upon the earlier phases of their lives.
The little incidents of childhood, interesting as they
may be to the psychologist, or within the family circle,
may be speedily set aside when there are ample
means of viewing the character under the clearer light
of its maturity.

The symmetry of the brief life of Edward Cracroft
Lefroy (born March 29, 1855, died September 19, 1891)
will be best seen by passing over the period of childhood,
touching rapidly on points of interest during the
twelve years of his school and college days, and dwell-
ing in any fulness only upon those latter years during
which, under the ever present shadow of death, his
poetical powers culminated, and the purity and strength
of his nature shone forth most brightly.

Born almost beneath the eaves of Westminster Abbey,
Lefroy was sent in very early years to a preparatory
school at Blackheath, whither his parents had lately
moved. Daily, as soon as school was over, he would

hasten home to pore over books after his own heart. It
was indicative of his later tastes that he founded a "Family
Magazine" in these earliest days, with himself as editor,
and a staff consisting of his sisters and a few intimate
friends; this publication would punctually appear—in
manuscript—at stated intervals. An ease and precision of
style are discernible even in these boyish productions.

It does not seem fanciful to trace to his family
antecedents Lefroy's strong leanings in early years
towards a life of letters, and, a little later on, towards
a life in the ministry. He was descended from a re-
fugee family who, to avoid religious persecution, came
over to this country from Flanders in 1587 and settled
in Canterbury. Three of his more immediate ancestors
on his father's side were successively rectors of Ashe in
Hampshire. The first of these, a Fellow of All Souls
College, Oxford, and of good social standing in his
neighbourhood, married Anne Brydges, a sister of Sir
Egerton Brydges, a man of considerable repute in his
day, and a writer of sonnets. Sir Egerton in his autobiography describes his sister, Mrs. Lefroy, in terms
of high admiration as "a woman of warm and rapid
poetical genius, whose conversation attracted all ears
and won all hearts." The nearest neighbours of the
Lefroys of Ashe were the Austens of Steventon, and so
it came about that Benjamin Lefroy, the last of the
three rectors of Ashe, married in 1814 Jane Anna
Elizabeth Austen, niece of Jane Austen the novelist.
On his mother's side, too, there was no lack of ability
of various kinds. In Sir John Franklin, the famous
Arctic explorer, Sir Willingham Franklin, puisne judge
of the Supreme Court of Madras, and in his aunt,
Sophia Cracroft, the clever and devoted companion of
Lady Franklin, Lefroy had examples of mental energy
and a spirit of self-sacrifice which may well have

encouraged him in the early determination he formed
to devote his life to the service of God, and by his
conduct and writings to elevate and improve the minds
of others.

In his twelfth year he was entered as a day boy at
the Blackheath Proprietary School, which the Rev. E. J.
Selwyn had recently raised to a high reputation. He
had been succeeded in the head-mastership by the Rev.
John Kempthorne, late Fellow of Trinity College,
Cambridge. During his school life (1866–1874).
Lefroy was rarely to be found among the foremost
either in form work or examinations. He was, however, well spoken of in the monthly reports, and such
masters as took the trouble—they were very few in
those days—to study individual character discovered in
him a quiet talent which might be allowed to diverge,
within reasonable limits, from the strait and narrow
way of classics and mathematics. Most of us who were
afterwards with him in the sixth form thought that he
could have shone in classics had he only cared. He
occasionally surprised head-master and boys alike by a
brilliant set of Greek or Latin verses, when the subject
happened to be congenial.

His friendships were few, but very close. He was
from the first an ardent entomologist, and possessed a
fair knowledge of botany. His great delight was to
wander on half-holidays with a chosen companion,
collecting butterflies. His home reading—as is common with boys of this temperament—was the chief
means of his education during this period. He carried
off the " Holiday Reading Prize " five years in succession, besides prizes for an English essay and an English
poem. From the year 1869 he was a frequent contributor to the school magazine—the *Blackheathen*—
which revived under his editorship in 1873. He wrote

constantly to the *English Mechanic* and *Science Gossip*.
The problem of heredity was one which early interested
him, and his letters in later years frequently deal with
this subject. His temperament at this time may be
described as a scientific curiosity combined with
poetical dreaminess. At an age when other boys were
struggling with the elements of the classics and the
first propositions of Euclid, Lefroy was absorbed in
Darwin's "Origin of Species," and soaring with Shelley
or Keats into impalpable spheres of spiritual beauty. It
is not surprising that his school work was neglected.
Referring in later years to this period he writes, "the
only excuse for me is that my bad health threw me out
of the ordinary groove, and made eccentric exertion
seem more delightful than ordinary work."

He matriculated in October 1874 at Keble College,
Oxford, where his early habits reasserted themselves.
Regret for indolence in school routine began indeed
to be felt, but occasional resolves to read for honours
were frustrated partly by continued delicate health,
and partly by his journalistic bias. When his college
tutor dissuaded him from the higher path he was at
first keenly disappointed, but soon found solace in the
manifold interests of University life and thought. The
most noticeable change in Lefroy at this time was the
rapid growth of his friendships. From being a shy and
retiring boy, sharing his tastes with a very few kindred
spirits, he suddenly found his chief interests in the
social life of the place. But these attractions did not
with him, as with many, tend to dissipate his intellectual purpose. They rather helped to show him
wherein his chief strength lay, and indicated to him the
means for its fuller development. His friends were
mostly men of literary tastes, but not bent on distinction in the Schools, nor curious to explore the unseen

foundations of the sciences. Their aim was rather to catch the inspiration of current thought and sentiment, to respond to the *genius loci*, and perhaps, by interchange of ideas, to hit upon some new *media via* which would satisfy the higher impulses of their nature without needlessly uprooting hereditary convictions.

On entering the University Lefroy formed the habit of keeping a diary—a habit which he continued, with a few years' break, to the end of 1883. During his undergraduate life the entries are very full and regular, describing University events, personal doings, the substance of discussions in societies of which he was a member, lists of books read and opinions formed upon them, and estimates—almost invariably kindly ones—of the characters of his many friends. The diaries are interspersed with photographs of his favourite buildings in Oxford. After taking his degree, Lefroy has less to record, his time being probably fully taken up in clerical work, and copious correspondence with his friends; but in the year 1883, following a serious illness and retirement from active duties, the diary is resumed in its fuller form. The judgments on men and books are more mature, and the cast of mind more contemplative than in the earlier records, though his human sympathies have lost none of their freshness. It is the picture of a peculiarly refined nature, mellowed and ennobled by suffering. The inner life of Lefroy could be written from these pages alone.

It must not be supposed that Lefroy's aim in keeping a diary was the sentimental pleasure of seeing himself as in a mirror, still less the desire that others should enjoy the spectacle after his death. The motives were doubtless mixed. He found a keen pleasure in the mere act of writing, and in expressing his thoughts in clear and precise language. But there was also an

element of self-discipline in the practice. He liked to
form definite opinions, and his pen became an almost
indispensable guide to his thoughts. The manifold
influences—intellectual and social—of a University life
tend to produce in some minds a state of unstable
mental equilibrium, and a chronic suspension of judgment. New ideas come too fast upon a mind weak in
fibre or lacking in moral earnestness. Lefroy's dis-
cursive reading and lively interest in all the intellectual
stir of Oxford life might have exposed him to some
such danger, had he not systematically habituated
himself to express his thoughts in writing. The
journalism which absorbed so much of his time as an
undergraduate also helped in the same direction. A
colleague on the Cambridge staff of the *Oxford and
Cambridge Undergraduates' Journal* wrote at this
period, " How I envy you your vocabulary and heaven-
born confidence ! You always seem to have an opinion,
whereas to me all sides of a question recommend themselves about equally, so that in an article I must sometimes affirm what I perhaps don't believe."

Lefroy was for some time editor of the above-named
Journal. I do not think that he was at his best in this
work. He had at this period two sides to his character,
—both strongly developed—the one a moral earnestness
and deep religious conviction, the other a keen critical
faculty and a sense of the ludicrous which at times
carried him into sarcasm. The best of his undergraduate articles were written in the former tone, but
where he tried to combine the two the results were
unfortunate. The collaboration of Mr. R. H. Hutton
and Mr. Labouchere would not produce more incon-
gruous results. There was a harmless undergraduate-
smartness in his vigorous tirade on tobacco-smoking
(Nicotinomania), but when he applied the same method

to the delicate subject of " Scepticism in Oxford," he
met with well-deserved attack. His college tutor, in a
subsequent talk with Lefroy, urged that satire and
ridicule were weapons which a Christian should never
employ, although admitting that the Marquis of
Salisbury, that " master of flouts and gibes," had once,
in conversation with him, justified their use in such
warfare. One suspects that the noble Marquis could
have made out a strong case for the practice by the aid
of Tertullian and a " Catena Patrum." These conflicting
elements in Lefroy's character, were, I think, the cause
of the impression which he produced upon some of
those outside his inner circle of friends—of a lack of
human sympathy, and perhaps a certain intellectual
pride, or aloofness. But the false note, if such it were,
was not sustained. The genial influence of college
friendships soon mellowed the tone. It was not that
the keenness of his critical powers became blunted, but
superficial smartness gave way to human sympathies ;
firmness of conviction did not turn to indifferentism,
but became blended with a delicate respect for types of
mind alien to his own. In his later years there was not
a trace of the old sarcasm. Any severity that remained
was directed against himself, not against others. If he
" touched a jarring lyre at first," he " ever strove to
make it true," and with the happiest results. There
was little in the life of Lefroy at the University which
calls for special notice. His friendships, with few exceptions, sprang from his connexion with the Union
Society, of which he became secretary and sub-librarian,
and his membership in the essay, literary and debating
societies of Keble College. His diaries are full of these
topics. One is impressed rather by the tone than the
substance of his reflexions. In times of the keenest
electioneering excitement at the Union, a friend's claims

are invariably preferred to his own, and the attitude of
an opponent is placed in the most generous light.

Lefroy felt some hesitation at first in joining the
Keble Literary Society, as its meetings were held on
Sunday evenings. His scruples, however, gave way to
the considerations that (1) "wines" and uproar were
less defensible, (2) frail human nature needed some
restorative from a system which required attendance at
three services every week-day, and four on Sundays,
(3) the dons approved of the society (!). Lefroy was
more at home in these gatherings than in the College
Debating Society. His temper at bottom, in spite of his
critical smartness, was too serious to find much pleasure
in arguing indifferently the *pros* and *cons* of a topic of
the day in a paradoxical vein. One of his best papers,
written for the Literary Society and since printed,
treated of "Spiritualism," in which he maintained with
much freshness the old theory that the phenomena
ascribed to the action of spirits may be the results of
some hitherto undiscovered natural law. The reading
of Swinburne's "Dolores" at one of these meetings
suggested to Lefroy the parody "Colores." I have
included it among the poems as an illustration of his
lighter vein.*

Lefroy was, as has been said, a copious contributor to
the *Oxford and Cambridge Undergraduates' Journal.* One
is not surprised at his tutor forbidding him to read for
Honours, when he is found writing forty-nine articles to
this magazine in a single term, with a Final Schools im-
pending. Yet he was, according to his own account, a
slow literary workman. "Inspiration seldom comes to
me. I never sit down suddenly and 'dash off' an article.

---

* Lefroy's later and, as I think, more characteristic style of
humour is seen best in the sonnets "A Philistine," "A philosopher," and "On a dull dog."

All my work is constructed in pieces, each laboriously hammered out, so that no one could tell by reading it how many sittings it took to finish any article. There is one advantage in this slow work—there is seldom any need of revision; also it does not excite the brain as inspiration does, and I might add that it fosters a feeling of self-reliance and confidence."

Several of these articles were reprinted in 1878, in a volume entitled " Undergraduate Oxford " (Slatter & Rose, Oxford). Their merit consists, I think, in their presenting the thoughtful conclusions of a cultivated and independent mind on many questions of current interest in the Oxford of that day. Lefroy mastered his facts with accuracy, and always offered a definite theory to his readers.

Reforms move so quickly nowadays, even in the Universities, that many of Lefroy's theories are no longer applicable, after twenty years, to the existing state of things. A few extracts may, however, be of interest. It will be noted that they are, in the main, conservative in tone.

Discussing the purposes and justification of Fellowships, in view of the then approaching Royal Commission, Lefroy discountenances Original Research Fellowships as unproductive in results and a luxury which an impoverished chest cannot afford, and he dislikes Prize Fellowships as creating an unhealthy stimulus to what should be a disinterested love of learning. He suggests that some, at least, should be " diverted, as recently at New College," to augmenting Scholarship funds, since " undergraduates have the first claim upon all endowments thus set free." (Perhaps some old College Statutes would be found to question this assertion.) He would retain certain Clerical Fellowships (at the risk of their forming ignoble inducements

to take Orders, a risk which he thinks is not so great
now as it was once), partly in order to ensure the
perpetuation of religious life in the colleges, and partly
because, in his view, if Clerical Fellowships die out,
college patronage should logically be handed over to
the Bishop of the Diocese, and the last link which
connects the University with the Church would thus be
severed.   The logical inference is not, I think, obvious,
for in recent years colleges have, with eminent success,
not unfrequently appointed to their livings able men
on their Boards who have not been Fellows.

On "The Endowment of Research" Lefroy's
position is fairly tenable, if his premises be granted
that Culture rather than the advance of science is the
raison d'être of a University.   With some exaggeration
he maintains that "research is generally employed in
demonstrating the worthlessness of received opinions,
in pulling down some lordly edifice of dogma which the
intellect of past centuries has constructed, and in which
the souls of men through long generations have securely
dwelt.   All metaphysical enquiries are practically useless, nor can philological researches, interesting as they
often are, merit the stimulus of extended endowments.
Men of learning already receive Professorships, Fellowships, &c., sufficient to supply leisure for independent
study.   What more can be reasonably demanded?"
Such further endowments, he continues, can only come
from one of two sources—(1) by the diverting of present
revenues from their ancient uses (a course which
Lefroy has already deprecated), or (2) from national
taxation, which he thinks the Chancellor of the
Exchequer would be slow to encourage.

In the same spirit, writing on the Honour Schools of
Natural Science, and the proposed special degrees—
distinct from the B.A.—for graduates in this Faculty, he

assails the movement (1) on the ground of its utilitarian bearing upon the medical profession (the aim of a University being rather to impart general culture than technical information), and (2) as tending, by the probable abolition of a compulsory modicum of classical study, to "destroy the cohesion of the undergraduate mass," and to draw its students from a lower grade of society.

In an article on "The Study of Classics," Lefroy restates with clearness and force the old arguments for their superiority as an instrument of education over a training in science or modern literature, concluding : "Humanity is the same to-day as ever. Its faculties, its needs, its aspirations are unchanged . . . . and culture must be sought in the study of the classics. . . . . When it can be proved that science and modern literature call forth the highest qualities of the mind, we will gladly hail them as efficient substitutes for the text-books of antiquity."

And what is this Oxford "Culture," this Aristotelian τέλος τέλειον, before which all other studies must bow the knee ? Lefroy attempts an answer to the question. He admits the difficulty of a definition. "Like some ethereal distillation in the alchymist's laboratory, it is too subtle to admit of minute analysis ; it resembles a perfume pervading the social atmosphere, which we cannot localise, or identify with any gross material particles. Perhaps we shall attain most nearly to the truth, if we call it not an object but the condition of an object. Culture, then, is the highest, purest and most perfect state to which our humanity in its threefold nature can be brought." After a paragraph in praise of Oxford athletics and physical training rather in the spirit of Plato than of Aristotle the germ of much which Lefroy afterwards expanded both in prose and verse —

he lays down "as an axiom, that culture, whether
bodily, mental or spiritual is not capable of progressive
development.   We cannot run or think better than an
accomplished Greek in Plato's time. . . . Our capacity
for holiness has remained unaltered since the days of
the Apostles ; our capacities for running and ratiocina-
tion since the remotest period to which historic
knowledge extends.   Evidently then, modern civilisa-
tion and modern discoveries have had no beneficial
effect upon culture—at least in the direction of upward
progress.   Indeed, by widening the field of knowledge,
they have made it harder to realise the refinement and
equipoise of faculties which are the essence of culture."
. . . . The University "might spend her revenues in
giving scientific lectures to the great unwashed : she
might subsidise social science congresses, and invent
schemes for the disposal of sewage . . . . but these
are not and never can be the objects for which Universities were founded, and certainly they do not tend
in the direction of culture. . . . . The heritage of all
times, to all time it will endure the same . . . .
because the capacity being unaltered, the method and
result of its perfection must be unchanged.   With the
common language which culture supplies, men may
converse across the centuries ; it is the only means by
which the present can join hands with the past.   (The
natural sciences would surely dispute this monopoly.)
. . . . It is this attitude of respect towards the learning
of the past which makes the Oxford of to-day a power
in the world.   It is the peculiar glory of this culture
that it can energise as well in the city as in the cloister,
in society as in solitude. . . . . Let Oxford men remember this, and they will do more to make their
University popular among the people than a dozen Royal
Commissions. . . . . *Spartam nactus es, hanc exorna.*"

It would be easy to criticise much of the above, and the more easy because Lefroy always commits himself to a definite, and therefore an assailable position. It is true that he could not have claimed—indeed he would certainly have disavowed—a first-hand acquaintance with some of the subjects of study upon which he passes an opinion. For example, I do not find that he ever attended any course of philosophical lectures, which could justify him in pronouncing upon the value of Oxford metaphysical studies. He had no taste or aptitude for such subjects. In classical scholarship his judgment was sound, and his study of ancient literature was continued long after he left Oxford. But the verbal analysis of the classics for the purpose of comparative grammar and philology was repugnant to his literary and poetic instincts. It must, however, be admitted that he misconceives the scope and methods of "Research." Its negative aspect is clearly subsidiary to its constructive side.

His strictures on Schools of Science and Medicine must be read solely in the light of his idea of the purposes of a University. Personally, Lefroy was by no means wanting in scientific sympathies, as is clear from his constant study of Darwin's works. Indeed, in later years he would frequently urge his clerical friends to shun controversies and word-wrangling, and recover their minds' health by a practical course in a laboratory. But allowing for some immaturity in his views, Lefroy's warning, even after the lapse of twenty years, is not without its value. The rapid advance of the practical sciences, their ever-growing claims to representation in an already overcrowded curriculum, the modern tendency to sacrifice the substance to the form (as seen in the extravagant insistence on *methodology*— barren word!—theories and "science of education"

&c.), all this makes it more than ever imperative that
we should formulate anew a definite answer to the
question, " What is the idea of a University ? " Some
may be pardoned for entertaining a doubt whether the
solution really lies in the development within its walls
of dissecting rooms and mechanical workshops, in
lectures on scientific farming, or even in the " quiet (?)
time " periodically provided for peripatetic " exten-
sionists," to whom a *bare month's* programme is offered
sufficiently varied indeed for the most omnivorous
appetite, but hardly representative in topics or treat-
ment of that solid learning which has made the Universities what they are.   There may be something,
after all, in the less ambitious ideal which our " rude
forefathers " kept steadily in view—that they should be
quiet seed plots,* where minds should be *slowly*
matured, characters moulded, and tastes formed which
the after-shocks of a material and mercantile world
might not have power to " utterly abolish or destroy."

> " Why with such earnest pains dost thou provoke
>   The years to bring the inevitable yoke,
>   Thus blindly with thy blessedness at strife ? "

For there *is* a real danger lest the democratic utili-
tarianism of these days should profane the calm
sanctuary of Letters and Art. The dread of being
thought " behind the age " may sometimes obscure
the deeper truth that it is the duty of a University to
be ahead of the age, a duty which she can only perform

---

* Recent attacks on the compulsory study of Greek point in
the same direction of decadence, it being held by many that
nowadays students of science have neither the time, nor the
need, to master the structure and contents of a language
which has trained the intellect and taste of three centuries of
Cambridge men.

by a comparative disregard of the restless swing of the popular pendulum. And if it be true, as a high authority has warned us, that the onward progress of scientific discovery cannot be indefinitely maintained, from what source can the pure and undefiled stream of Letters and learning be again replenished, if the Pierian spring itself be choked by the dust and detritus of matter?

It is gratifying to find at the present moment (Feb. 15, 1896) the Professor of Poetry in the University of Oxford, Mr. W. J. Courthope, justifying "the study of classical literature as pursued by the English Universities in a spirit different alike from the Italian humanists, who regarded the ancients as the model of abstract form, and from that of the German Universities, which regarded the ancient languages as a department of abstract knowledge. *We* had looked on classical literature as the finest school of taste, and the education of taste itself as a means to a practical, a "political" end. . . . . Year by year the Universities sent to the Bar, the public services, and to Journalism large numbers of young men who helped to form public opinion. . . . . We shall be looking in the right direction if we take for our standard (of good taste) the principle which Pericles recommended to the Athenians —φιλοσοφοῦμεν ἄνευ μαλακίας—we pursue Culture in a manly spirit."

An essay on "Slithy Toves" treats of Boat-captains and the joys of football. It is the key to much of Lefroy's later Christian-Hellenism. He realises in vivid language the physical sensations of the football hero,[*] and traces in his sport the clue to that quality which goes by the name of "British pluck."

In the ideal Boat-captain he sees the embodiment of

---

[*] Compare the Sonnet " A football player."

authority, self-control, tact, and social gifts,* and ad-
mires the instinct which leads the flower of England's
youth to submit to the ruling of their chosen leader
with unquestioning docility.

It was not merely the admiration of physical symmetry, strength, health and comeliness—in short of
the τὸ καλόν—which attracted Lefroy. These qualities
seemed to him also to form the natural foundation
of a genuine morality and a healthy religion. Lefroy
was possessed of an ineradicable conviction that the
true hero and saint—the terms were for him almost
synonymous—might be moulded on a basis of naturalism out of strong animal impulses and perfect physical
development, as well as out of pain, disease and self-
imposed limitations.

To harmonise the antagonistic principles of Christianity and Hellenism in this matter is doubtless impossible. The problem, in fact, existed before either creed
was formulated, though Christianity, partly by its in-
herent principles, but more by its overgrowth of asceticism, has accentuated it, and it may be noted that the
controversy has re-arisen on every occasion of the revival of letters. In its more personal and common-
place aspect, it presents itself to every man in the
form : " May I not indulge my clearly natural instincts
—bodily appetite, anger, self-love, etc. ? "

The vague generalisation offered by the Modern
Hedonist in answer to such inquiries—that man is meant
for self-expression rather than for self-elimination—did
not wholly satisfy Lefroy. He saw the problem very
clearly from the varying points of view of the artist, the
scholar and the moralist, and thus realised the difficulties
more vividly than most men. He was keenly alive to

* See the Sonnet " A palæstral study."

the beauty and *abandon* of Hellenic naturalism, he appreciated the charm of classical literature, and was in sympathy with some of the theories of life and society which Plato and Aristotle constructed upon this basis.

This, and much more, contributed to form his pagan sympathies, and to engender in him an antipathy to the accretions with which historical Christianity had overlaid the true human ideal—its maimed and world-renouncing asceticism, its metaphysical wranglings, its petty party strifes, its hollow conventionalities, and the rigid and arbitrary boundary lines which it drew between the world and the Church, the spirit and the flesh.

When Dean Burgon levelled his famous indictment against the Oxford of that time—for ardent reformers think that progress cannot be healthily at work unless it sets in their own peculiar direction—that morality in the University was rotten at the core and religion was fast decaying, Lefroy was content characteristically to reply that "the rowing element alone would suffice to keep our social system strong, pure and manly."

In "Muscular Christianity," a paper read before the Keble Essay Club, and afterwards reprinted (Slatter & Rose, Oxford, 1877), Lefroy discusses the two leading ideals of life, the Hellenic and the Hebraic, and maintains that Muscular Christianity combines the good points of both. He criticises the aspect of Hellenism, which he attributes to the teaching of Mr Symonds and Mr. Pater—'Act according to the promptings of nature, and you cannot go wrong.' "Is the term 'nature,'" he asks, 'Anglo-Byzantine' (as Mr. Tyrwhitt would say) for the worst passions and most carnal inclinations of humanity? I fear that there is too much reason to dread an affirmative answer." But Lefroy thinks better of the old Greeks. "Bodily development was much to them, but spiritual and intellectual development was more. They knew, as well as the great Apostle of the Gentiles, that unrestrained indulgence in fleshly appetites must end in degradation and death. Τὸ καλόν, τὸ πρέπον, these terms express an aspiration to the highest and most perfect life of which they could conceive." It is to be feared that Lefroy is here idealising the Greek ideal.

He next discards that modern view of Hellenism which regards it as practically equivalent to asceticism.

" Hebraism is our conception of the Jewish spirit, and that conception is probably much exaggerated. . . . . We have formed a certain idea of ancient Jewish temperament, derived mainly from traditional sources, and chiefly due to Michael Angelo and his brother artists. But if we read the Old Testament with an unprejudiced mind . . . we might detect in the Jewish character more culture, more refinement, and more appreciation of natural beauty, than we have hitherto given it credit for. But," as he goes on to observe, "the Hebraism with which we are concerned is not the temperament of an ancient nation but a supposed attribute of modern Christianity." And here, again, he doubts whether there was much of this in the Christianity of the Apostles, and in the early (Lefroy must mean the very early) Church. " It is difficult to see what warrant can be found in Scripture for asceticism or religious hysteria." Accepting with reservation Kingsley's view of Muscular Christianity in his well-known University Sermon, as a religion which does not "exalt the feminine virtues to the exclusion of the masculine," Lefroy concludes : " It is emphatically the religion of youth. In life there is an age of discipline, an age of energy, an age of meditation.

Muscular Christianity meets a man in the age of discipline, and carries him into the age of energy. It does not leave him then, but its chief work has been accomplished : it becomes more a temper of mind, less an impulse of action. . . . Muscular Christianity includes all that is brightest in Hellenism, and all that is purest in Hebraism. It involves the cultivation of every faculty, the use of every talent. It is the best safeguard against the sin of intolerance and bigotry, for it will keep body, soul and intellect in stable equilibrium, and equilibrium means moderation.

" The Muscular Christian can conquer anything—even the Church Association and Lord Penzance, for he can rise superior to Arches Courts and chasubles, Privy Councils and copes. He will view our great Ideal in an aspect full of strength and beauty, an aspect, perhaps, too little seen. He will view Him as that Leader of men, Himself a man, whose faithful soldier and servant he has promised to be ; as the Leader, the Worker, the Friend ; not the Christ of the painted window, not the Christ of the marble shrine, but that Being of Whom, in the supremest hour of His earthly life, no truer description could be found than this— *Ecce Homo !* "

I sent Mr. Addington Symonds, at his request, a copy of Lefroy's " Muscular Christianity " after the death of the latter. " I should like to understand," he wrote, " his views upon the relation of Hellenism to Christianity. For myself, it is difficult enough to adjust Hellenism to modern ideas. Nothing which Lefroy said, even were it severe stricture of my own writings (in the 'Studies of the Greek Poets,' &c.), would break the impression which he has made upon me. I am not a dogmatist, but a perplexed seeker, whom length of life has made diffident." In the fuller notice of Lefroy's work, which his own death prevented, it was Symonds's intention to compare his own and Lefroy's aspects of Hellenism with especial reference to the circumstances which evoked Lefroy's pamphlet. I cannot but think that a more careful study of Symonds's teaching would have led Lefroy to modify some of the strictures contained in his paper. Christianity could certainly find little to criticise in the tone of Symonds's reply to me after reading the pamphlet. " I fully understand," he writes, " what he felt about Pater and me. In fact it (the paper) recalls vividly an attack which a Mr. Tyrwhitt made upon my morals at a time when he thought I might be elected to the Chair of Modern Poetry at Oxford . . . . I am undoubtedly open to criticism. And it is just for this reason that I welcome Lefroy so much, because at heart he was at one with me, but in him 'the elements were kindlier mixed,' the spirit purer."

It was this blend of Hellenic with Christian sentiment which kept Lefroy during his University life equally apart from Ritualists and Evangelicals. On the opening of the new chapel at Keble he writes that the majority of the men are so high in their Church views that he trembles lest this event should be made the signal for " the introduction of all sorts of ecclesiastical vagaries." But his own personal religion was meanwhile deepening through or in spite of this environment. In February 1875 he writes : " In my present state of mind, I should hardly care for existence, were it not for the hope and expectation of becoming a clergyman." " If I should ever get a church of my own, it would be my endeavour to link a choral service with an Evangelical sermon."

Of course Lefroy, like most thoughtful men at the Universities, came into contact at times with advanced opinions. Neither at this nor at any other period does he seem to have been much affected by their influence.

The difficulties which he felt before Ordination were rather those of personal unworthiness. "I feel that I can always argue with sceptics in perfect safety. The evidence in favour of Christianity is one which is within the heart, and is not assailable from without. It is useless for any one to prove to me that the operation of natural laws precludes the answering of prayer, because I know that such is not the case by my own experience."

Both at Oxford and throughout his life, Lefroy appears as a man of strong and well-defined character, which, while always open to new aspects of truth, was rarely in danger of suffering even a temporary eclipse of faith or a weakening of early convictions.

It must not be inferred from any criticism which he passed upon the attitude of some of its extreme members that Lefroy was insensible of the debt which he personally owed to Keble College. The present Sub-Warden, the Rev. W. Lock, Lefroy's tutor, wrote on hearing of his death : " I was always much interested in his literary work. His health, while with us, really prevented him doing himself justice. . . . Many of his contemporaries had a high opinion of his powers and character." Lefroy acknowledges his deep obligation to his college most fully in the Preface to " Undergraduate Oxford." His happiest and healthiest days were spent there. In his article " A Young College " he refers with pride to the fact that " while the proportion of students who took honours in other colleges was thirty per cent., the proportion of Keble undergraduates was rather over sixty per cent." Its principle of " plain living " calls forth his warmest praise. " Not a day too soon was this concrete protest made against the growing tendency towards extravagant living, not only in Oxford, but in the country at large." " What Keble College does with exemplary

energy (Lefroy was a true Baconian in maintaining the
'fruits-philosophy') is worth far more than a thousand
empty lamentations on the extravagance and recklessness
of the age." But he reserves his highest admiration for
Keble College in that she is a standing condemnation of
the educational theories of the secularist, and a living
" witness to the vitality of the Church of England.
'There has arisen in these later days,' to quote the
words of Lord Salisbury spoken last term (Easter term,
1876), 'a school of men who have not so much differed
from us in that they profess any religious opinion, on
which we do not agree, as in that they speak of religion
as a thing which to a University should not be a matter
of importance. Some have held the language that
religion has little business in any University at all ; they
have contended that Universities and Colleges are lay
Corporations, and from that they have drawn this curious
inference—justifiable only on the supposition that laymen
have nothing to do with religion—that religion is no
business of theirs ! Against all such theories of this
kind Keble College is a standing protest . . . . We are
sometimes told that systems of negative philosophy are
becoming the most prominent influences of the present
day. We do not believe it, partly because it is not in
human nature to rest satisfied with negatives, but chiefly
because negatives cannot exert any influence at all . . . .
When the believers in negative philosophies have
founded such a College as Keble they will have more
claim to the consideration of practical men than they
have at present.' 'But,' as the Chancellor remarked,
'they never seem to get so far as undertakings of that
kind. They have no good news, no evangel to offer,
and naturally they will make no sacrifice to offer it.' "

CHAPTER II

Urbs caelestis, urbs beata,
Super petram collocata,
Urbs in portu satis tuto,
De longinquo te saluto—
Te saluto, te suspiro,
Te affecto, te requiro.
                    HILDEBERT.

We live in a world which is full of misery and ignorance, and the plain duty of each and all of us is to try and make the little corner he can influence somewhat less miserable and somewhat less ignorant than it was before he entered it.—HUXLEY.

AFTER taking his B.A. degree in June, 1877, Lefroy spent the summer in touring through Norway. There was a good deal of rough work in such an excursion twenty years ago, and for a delicate man Lefroy displayed remarkable energy. In the autumn he took a private tutorship in Scotland, and when this was over, he set his face steadily towards the Church, which we have seen was the profession he had deliberately chosen some years previously.

Feeling that he needed some more special preparation than Oxford or even Keble College had offered, and doubtless attracted by the religious activity then breaking out in the Church in Cornwall, under the inspiring influence of Dr. Benson, then in the first year

of his Episcopate at Truro, Lefroy entered as a student
of the Truro Theological College in January, 1878.   He
was hardly the man likely to derive much benefit from
the routine of a clergy training school, and he seems to
have missed the ampler air of Oxford.   His chief
pleasures he found in the daily services and choral
singing of the Cathedral, and the main benefit he carried
away was the lasting friendships formed with a few of
his fellow-students.   Some of his happiest recollections
in after years were the personal relations into which he
had been brought with the Bishop and his staff.   Most of
Lefroy's correspondence during this period—and he was
an indefatigable letter writer—turns upon the attitude
of different schools in the Church.   His early Evangelicalism had been largely qualified by the influence of
Keble College.   And not only was he attracted by the
activity of the High Church party (statistics conclusively
proving to him the striking results of their work in
London alone during the last preceding decade), but he
considered that their tenets were more in accordance
with the spirit of the Book of Common Prayer.   He
would not admit that it was any argument against a
doctrine or a practice to say that it was " Popish."
" Almost every doctrine and practice of the English
Church is Popish."   As for confession, he will accept
what the Prayer Book teaches, neither more nor less.
But with Ritualism he feels no sympathy.   He subsequently refused a curacy offered at Truro because he
would have to wear coloured stoles, " cream coloured on
high festivals, violet in Lent, red on martyrs' days, and
green at all other times."   On the other hand he has
little in common with those who would dispense with all
external aids to worship.   He shrinks from accepting a
title at an Evangelical church in a London suburb
because he would " certainly have favoured the faction

which desires to surplice the choir and abolish evening Communions." He also wishes not to expose himself to the temptation of pulpit display which a fashionable parish might offer, and he seriously inclines towards Helston in Cornwall, as presenting no such worldly allurements. Picturing his life spent and ended there, he writes to a friend, enclosing a sketch of a simple slab in Helston church with the inscription " E. C. L. His ambition died, Trinity Sunday, 1878."

While Lefroy thus seems to be chiefly concerned with externals—with the discovery of a practical *via media* between Anglicanism and Evangelicalism, he was not blind to the deeper problems of the age. He will not allow, as a lady friend suggests, that the clergy are simply bigoted, or blind to the intellectual difficulties of the time. They see them as clearly as other men, but they surmount them by other than intellectual means. On the eve of his Ordination (March, 1878) he writes to a friend : " If a man wishes to live a base, pleasure-seeking life, or indeed any life below the highest possible to him, he naturally begins by denying the existence of a God. One thing seems quite clear to me, with very rare exceptions. The Christians are the only people who try to live up to what is admitted on all hands to be the highest ideal. Listen to a young undergraduate Neologist waxing eloquent about the beauty of heroism, self-sacrifice, benevolence, philanthropy and the like, and then inquire what he *does* in these several directions. Nothing ; on the contrary, by his luxury and selfishness, he contradicts his professed principles. Not long since, a friend wrote to me denying our Lord's Divinity, but praising Him as the great Exemplar to be imitated by all. Yet I have never observed a conscious effort on his part to become more like Christ. Such men delude themselves and the world. Why don't they speak out and say boldly, 'We are Hedonists, we live only to gratify the body and the less noble appetites. We don't care a farthing for heroism, philanthropy and virtue, such things don't pay'? This may be the last opportunity I may have of saying such things from the 'disinterested' standpoint of a layman. Henceforth I will argue no more. Divine wisdom shall not strive and cry in the person of her priests."

I think Lefroy must have been lately reading the peroration of the capital sermon in "Tristram Shandy"— "Whenever a man talks loudly against religion, always suspect that it is not his reason but his passions which have got the better of his creed. A bad life and a good belief are disagreeable and troublesome neighbours; and where they separate, depend upon it 'tis no other cause but quietness' sake."

Still, it is no disparagement to Lefroy's intellect to suggest that such difficulties as he may have felt then or at other times in the Christian religion were mainly practical. He never questioned, so far as I can discover, the reality of the Christian revelation, the Divinity of our Lord, the inspiration of the Scriptures, the efficacy of the Sacraments, the personal in-dwelling of the Spirit. He was constitutionally proof, I think, against any sceptical attacks upon the vital doctrines of the Christian Church. The problem to him was rather whether the Christian ideal corresponded, and gave adequate scope, to the natural instincts of a healthy-minded man—in other words, to adopt his favourite standpoint, whether Christian-Hellenism was a paradox or a possibility. This problem, which occupied him chiefly in the days of his health, gave place later, as is the way of such perplexing problems, to the more pressing one, 'Can Christian faith, in actual experience, break the shock of prolonged suffering, and finally triumph over pain ? ' The last ten years of Lefroy's own life were one prolonged answer in the affirmative to this crucial question. *Solvitur ferendo.*

A philosophy, still more a religion, of doubt was thus not merely uncongenial to Lefroy's temperament, but carried with it its own greatest condemnation in his eyes, that it blunted the edge of action. He keenly realised how much men lose that is valuable while they wait for their intellectual convictions to be fully satisfied. Writing to the same friend he tells him : " I have concluded that in order to do a good day's work it is justifiable to squelch one thousand doubts. St. Augustine nobly says ' et *nos* vincamus *aliquid* '—why not our doubts ? Depend upon it, the doubtfulness *that hinders* arises from physical or moral, not *intellectual* causes. I cannot understand how it is that you allow your inherited bias to trick you in all kinds of ways and assume the garb of ' pure reason.' " (Nov. 21, 1882). And again : " There is but one answer to your philosophy of doubt. *Elect* a creed. None will ever elect *you*. To wait for conviction is the part of a dreamer. Modify, limit, expand as you may have occasion, but you *must* begin with something ready made to your hand. It is ridiculous to suppose that any single man can arrive at absolute truth.—(J. H. Newman's argument.) . . . . You speak of building your own platform, of putting together the facts of which you feel experimentally sure. You had much better take *Christ*, and make *Him* the corner-stone of your edifice. Christ is the only God, the only religion, the only life, which can satisfy souls like yours and mine. I realise it more every day." (Oct. 23, 1880.)

Inspiring words like these were written to not a few of Lefroy's friends, who opened their hearts to him at perplexing crises of their lives. If they did not always follow the advice which was offered, they could not fail

to be stirred by the earnestness which sprang straight
from personal conviction, and to be touched by the sympathy, discrimination and infinite pains with which Lefroy
was ever ready at the call of friendship or distress.

We have seen above (p. 23) that Lefroy was so
deeply convinced, by personal experience, of the independent reality of the spiritual life that he anticipa-
ted little danger to it from any assaults made under the
cover of physical science. Consistently with this attitude, he doubted whether the cause of Christianity
would be permanently advanced or strengthened by
drawing Science into an artificial alliance with Religion.
In this spirit he comments as follows on Drummond's
"Natural Law in the Spiritual World." "It is well
written, suggestive, and full of happy illustrations. Mr.
Drummond's position is this, 'Admitting the truth of
Mr. H. Spencer's system of physical *laws*, how can we
restate our old religious beliefs so as to make those laws
operative in the spiritual world?' Now, for my own
part, I don't feel at all certain that Mr. Spencer is
invariably a safe guide in scientific matters, and more-
over I can't perceive why it should be thought that the
laws of Biology have anything to do with the life of the
soul. . . . . I believe that such books do good because
they set people thinking. But I am not inclined to
study them myself, for my feeling is that all attempts
to draw elaborate analogies and parallels between the
physical and spiritual spheres must be vain and fallacious.
They have no more value than the famous chrysalis-
and-butterfly illustration of the immortality of the soul
—pretty as imagery, worthless as evidence. I don't
believe it possible to get material proof of any spiritual
truth." (Sept., 1884.)

I have described at some length what I conceive to
have been Lefroy's mental attitude on entering the

ministry, as it seems to me to be of more general interest than any minute description of his actual clerical work. Indeed, the latter covers a very short period, and may be best told in his own brief and pathetic words: "Ordained to curacy, Old Lambeth Church, June, 1878. Ill and resigned, Nov., 1878. Curate of St. German's, Blackheath, Feb., 1879. Resigned (unwillingly) July, 1880. Curate of St John's, Woolwich, Sept., 1880. Ill and resigned, July, 1882." But his religious influence, as a man and a clergyman, was by no means confined to this short four years of work "in his Master's service." When illness had finally closed the days of official curacies, he still held the "cure of souls," in the largest sense, to be his first duty and the main object of such life as remained to him.

Lefroy has left but little record of his first curacy at Old Lambeth Church. One incident therein is preserved in his own words, and is worth quoting, if only as an illustration of the kindliness of the late Archbishop of Canterbury. "The episode occurred in the first weeks of my ministry, and afforded a good deal of amusement to a select circle, and was not, I hope, without its lesson for myself. The laugh at the time was no doubt *against* me, but after the lapse of some years I can afford to join in it as heartily as any one; and indeed I question whether I had any legitimate cause for shame even at the moment. I tell the story now, partly by way of a tribute to the memory of a great and good man, and partly because the experience may be useful to my younger brethren. When I was ordained (in the diocese of Rochester) the Bishop found a title for me in the mother parish of Lambeth. The rector was abroad for the benefit of his health, and I lived

with the senior curate at the rectory. At that time
the second Pan-Anglican Council was assembled, and
bishops from all quarters of the world were to be met
in the neighbourhood of the Archbishop's Palace.
These, with Dr. Tait himself, used to attend the
Sunday services at our church. Soon after my arrival
I was called upon to preach to this distinguished
company. I felt myself to be in an awkward predica-
ment. A young man of twenty-three, just ordained,
may be excused if he shrinks from homiletic exercises
in the presence of the Primate and a number of
spiritual peers. I could not screw up my courage so
far as to venture upon an original discourse. Modesty
or cowardice (I know not which) impelled me to fall
back upon some abler man than myself. I chose the
writer with whom I was best acquainted. It was
Frederick Robertson. Looking carefully through his
volumes, I selected the sermon on the 'New Com-
mandment of Love' as the one best suited to my
purpose. I copied it with various alterations and
omissions, and took it to Church. I thought it well
to acquaint my colleague with my purpose. It was
an evening service, and the congregation was good.
The Archbishop sat in his pew with his family and
episcopal guests. I preached the sermon with as much
vigour as I could manage. It sounded satisfactory,
and I descended from the pulpit fairly pleased with
the experiment. Dr. Tait gave the blessing from his
seat, the congregation dispersed, and I went home to
supper, thinking the whole matter at an end. Not so,
however. About nine o'clock a messenger arrived from
the palace, bearing a note for me in the Archbishop's
handwriting. It stated that a controversy had arisen
at the palace which I alone could allay. Was the
sermon just preached by me my own or another

man's, or partly my own and partly another's? 'Pray
excuse this' (added his Grace) 'from one old enough
to be your father or grandfather,' and he invited me
to come round and explain the mystery by word of
mouth. I was too much ashamed of myself to do
this. But while the messenger waited I wrote a short
note giving an account of my discourse, and of the
motives which prompted me to borrow it. Twenty
minutes later the messenger returned with a second
missive of the kindest possible character. 'Do not'
(said the Archbishop) 'allow yourself to be the least
annoyed by my note. I should like, when I can get
a moment's time, to have a talk with you about the
difficulties of preaching on such an occasion as to-night.'"
(An invitation to dine the next night followed, which
Lefroy accepted.) "I found myself placed at the table
beside a venerable dean, who told me that my letter
of the previous evening had been read aloud by the
Archbishop, and that the company assembled agreed
that my defence was a good one. He was kind enough
to compliment me on the delivery of the sermon. He
said, 'I was the one to suspect you; I know Robertson's sermons well; but I had some difficulty in
persuading the others that you were not reading your
own words; you threw so much spirit into them.'
This compliment was not disagreeable; and after
dinner Dr. Tait himself came up to me in a corner
of the drawing-room, and gave me some friendly
counsel. The gist of it was that I had better not
copy from the open book, no matter how much I
altered, but having read the sermon and got the pith
of it in my head, I might then reproduce it in my own
language: he saw no objection to that; he rather
thought the process would be educational."

The episode hardly calls for comment. The Archbishop, it will be noted, with all the circumstances before him, held the moral aspect of the case to turn on the distinction between an open and a closed book of reference.

In the spring of 1879, his health having somewhat improved, Lefroy resumed work as curate of St. German's (proprietary chapel), Blackheath. The last vicar, the Rev. H. Martyn Hart, now Dean of Denver, Colorado, had gained some celebrity as a preacher. A man of scientific, as well as general culture, he had presented Evangelical doctrine in a popular and forcible manner. The sphere was congenial to Lefroy. While not failing to impress the older members of the congregation by their earnestness and literary grace, his sermons proved especially attractive to young men. Cadets from Woolwich Academy, boys from the Greenwich Naval College and Blackheath School, students from the numerous army coaching establishments round about, and a large number of young business men were drawn to this earnest and ascetic-looking preacher, who seemed to understand their daily thoughts and interests, and, while making allowance for their failings, to lift them into a purer air, and, appealing to their better instincts, to awake in them a love for the beauty of holiness.

But Lefroy's influence extended far beyond the pulpit. Woolwich balls, Greenwich messes, football matches, whist parties in his lodgings, smoking concerts at crammers' houses, and visits to the theatre were quietly utilised by Lefroy—not for evangelising, but for frank and kindly interchange of thought between man and man, which might at least disarm the prejudices so often expressed against the wearer of the black coat, but really directed against the principles which he professes. Writing about this to a clerical friend, he says : " Whether or no the end justified the proceeding, there may be a difference of opinion. But I am quite sure that young men of the educated classes can only be got at in the way I have adopted. . . . . Living as you do among a naturally religious people, you can hardly realise how much religion is losing its hold upon educated men in London. When I say ' religion,' I mean traditional Christianity as it is commonly preached. Among all my young acquaintance, I hardly know one who implicitly holds to the faith in which he has been reared. . . . . Clergymen ought to be honest to their convictions, and they ought to keep themselves abreast with the thought of the day. If they did this, the rising generation would not be alienated from them as I fear it is " (Dec. 18, 1879).

Though Lefroy did not underrate the importance of his profession as a clergyman, he seems to have felt keenly the limitations which it imposed on his practical usefulness. " A parson can do so very little compared with a layman. Were I a real soldier, I should not be less a Christian than I am. On the contrary, I should have an opportunity of *showing* that I am one, which is denied me now—it being taken for granted. And oh ! I *should* like to get out of these black garments, symbols of a sacerdotalism which is alien to the bent of my mind. It is one thing to be 'a soldier and servant of Jesus Christ' (which, God helping me, I will always try to be), and quite another to serve as officer of an ecclesiastical corporation, the constitution of which, and the official members of which, are in a great measure distasteful to me. *I* am to blame, not *it* or *they*, but still the fact remains " (Oct. 17, 1879).

It was, however, always with a reservation that Lefroy accepted the title of Broad Churchman. " Broad Churchman too often means nothingarianism, or at least a belief that all creeds are equally true or equally false. And when a *young man* declares himself a Broad Churchman, the chances are that he has no religion at all. A man must be *religious* before all things. When he is confirmed in religion, then it will be time enough for him to weigh dogmas and dissect creeds . . . . I do not say that Broad Churchism *could not* lead a man to religion, but it does not as a rule. We have a visible Church, and an open Bible; when a man has learned all that these can teach him, when he has taken up his cross, and is striving earnestly to follow the Divine Master, then he may call himself what he will. . . . . You may ask what I mean by 'being religious.' Well, there are three qualities at least which go to form a religious spirit; reverence—a high estimate of goodness outside us; humility—a lowly estimate of ourselves; zeal—love in action " (Oct., 1878).

Lefroy frequently deplores the onesidedness of a parson's training. In the following letter he hits a defect which has been sadly overlooked in this age of reforms. The leaders of the Church show no signs of moving in the matter. It is much to be wished that the intelligent laity in the Church would come to the relief of their distressed clerical brethren. The subject to which I refer is the character of Bishops' examinations for candidates for Holy Orders. " What is the use of cramming such books as Pearson on the Creed, or Paley's Evidences? Our age has got beyond them. They were useful in their day, but that (*me judice*) is long past. Even Waterland and Hooker are unfitted for modern examinations. The time spent upon them might, I think, be better bestowed on Biblical exegesis, or ethical enquiries " (Feb., 1880).

I think there is very little doubt that many able and

religious men are repelled from taking Orders by the antiquated and dogmatic character of the works which confront them at the very threshold of a clerical career.

And once again, on the intellectual equipment of the clergy : " My theory is that every parson should be great at some non-professional study. He should be a classic, mathematician, poet, historian, essayist, scientist, naturalist or antiquary. Thus he will gain recreation for himself, and credentials with the world at large " (Feb., 1880).

Writing later on the same subject, Lefroy will not admit that " a clergyman wastes his times in getting up a branch of science." " It is the most useful kind of recreation he can employ himself in. You say ' I want results only—the fruit of other men's thinking.' Well, but you can't weigh and appreciate results, unless you have had a scientific training yourself. And what is more, the educated laity won't believe in your science, unless they know that you have really gone into the matter with thoroughness. So much bad science is babbled from the pulpit that the clever layman has grown suspicious. You must be a B.Sc., or an F.R.S. before he will credit you. For my part, I used to avoid all science in my sermons, knowing that I know next to nothing about it. I wish all the brethren were equally reticent " (Aug., 1885).

When urging a member of a theological college to a London degree ("for a man who can write himself 'M.A. London' is *nulli secundus*"), he adds : " I would abolish every theological college in the land, unless they would either pass their men through London, or take none but graduates " (Nov., 1880).

These were not haphazard utterances of Lefroy, but the outcome of his personal experience. He held that any religious influence to be effective must come from,

and appeal to the *whole* man. It was thus that he won
his way into the hearts of his hearers He spoke "as
to wise men," and was valued accordingly.

Lefroy's health gave way again in July, 1880, and he
was unwillingly compelled to withdraw from his work
at St. German's for a short rest. In September, however, he resumed clerical duties at St. John's, Woolwich.
The congregation here was of a more composite
character than that of St. German's, Blackheath, which
had consisted almost entirely of well-to-do people. He
threw himself into the parochial life of the place—its
Sunday schools, its science classes, &c.—heart and
soul. I have before me many touching letters from the
humbler members of the congregation, all pointing to
the personal interest which he took in the daily lives of
those of whom he had charge. His vicar, the Rev. J.
Oxenham Bent, has kindly recorded for me his own
impressions of Lefroy. "His thoughtful sermons were
characterised by a lucid style, good delivery, practical
teaching and manly tenderness which found their way
to the hearts of the congregation—his intense feeling
and very impressive look and manner gave a singular
pathos to his words. . . . . Well do I remember his
sermons upon the texts "Lord help me," "We all do
fade as a leaf," "So He giveth his beloved sleep."
Oftentimes there was a tone of sadness in his sermons
and conversation, yet he had, nevertheless, a keen sense
of humour. The secrets of Lefroy's good influence
were, first, I think, his gentle strength of character,
and his refined mind, enshrined in a delicate body, and
his poetic temperament, which was appreciated by us in
warlike, and, shall we say rather, prosaic Woolwich?
Secondly, his large-hearted sympathy with the strong
as well as with the weak, and his keen interest alike in
the athletic games, and in the moral and intellectual

advancement of young men. Thirdly, and—may we not
say chiefly?—his high purpose and devout Christian
aim; and the impression which he always gave, that
his thoughts were on the borderland, and that his
habit was to look trustingly upward—if he sighed, he
still looked up Of his great kindness to me, and of his
genial loyalty and personal friendship, I could not fully
speak."

At the end of nearly two years' work in this parish, in
the summer of 1882, Lefroy received a serious warning
from an eminent London physician on his state of
health. Of that I shall say more in the next chapter.
It was a heavy blow to him to have to abandon the
parish to which he had become so endeared. The congregation presented him, on parting, with a testimonial
expressing their warm gratitude, and the deep sense of
their loss.

After a year of great bodily prostration, we find
Lefroy keenly interesting himself in matters affecting
the welfare of the Church, although no longer able to
bear an active part in her work. A few extracts, taken
at random, may close this chapter. Lefroy's liberal
sympathies naturally extended to other Christian de-
nominations. The outburst of *odium theologicum* in
certain quarters against the appointment of Mr. R. F.
Horton to be an Examiner in elementary Divinity at
Oxford in 1883 arouses his indignation. "He was my
contemporary at Oxford, and a man worthy of all
possible honour. As a scholar, as an athlete, as a
speaker, he stood high in everybody's esteem. He
was captain of his college boat club, and did wonders
for its prestige on the river. . . . . He was President
of the Union. . . . . His pleasant manner made him
popular in all circles. Yet he never sought to disguise
is ardent attachment to the Gospel of Christ. . . . .

And when Horton gained his fellowship, there was no alteration in his conduct. He decided to enter the Independent ministry. . . . . And this is the man who may not be allowed to examine undergraduates in the xxxix Articles, and the Bible—that is, he may not do what any agnostic is allowed to do, so long as he does not blatantly proclaim his dissent from the Church of England! For my part, I believe Horton to be every whit as much a minister of Jesus Christ as I am myself, but if I did not, I should be very slow to vote against him when he sought an office allowed him by the law of the land " (Dec., 1883).

When the question of the presence of the bishops in the Upper House was being canvassed in the papers, Lefroy agreed with the *Guardian*, that it would not much matter if they did lose their seats there. He proceeds: "They do not give their votes with much discretion, as far as I can judge. The Peers are sufficiently conservative without them. And it is not pleasant to see them made 'buffers' between the Church and the world. Nor do I think their spiritual influence would suffer by some diminution of their temporal dignity. They would be more helpful to the clergy, I fancy, if they were not such 'awful' personages, in whose presence we all tremble" (Nov., 1884).

Lefroy frequently dwells on the question of disestablishment. He held strong opinions on the unwisdom of the clergy in entering the political arena in defence of the Church. "I think the clergy should, as far as possible, leave fighting to their lay allies. Much as I value the establishment, I value my position as a Christian minister still more, and I know very well that, if I were to play the political agitator, I should lose what influence I have with my Liberal friends, many of whom I greatly respect, and in some points agree with. Let us always remember that the Church of Christ is immensely broader, deeper and more important than the establishment. . . . . It would be easy to exaggerate the power of the clergy in politics. I believe it to be very small, even when exercised to the uttermost " (Dec., 1885).

Lefroy's respect for " The Fathers " seems to have been a qualified one. " It is often my duty to review some new edition of one of them for the *Guardian.* . . . I have now on hand Vincentius Lirinensis and Heurtley's collection of extracts ' De Fide et Symbolo.' . . . . All Patristic literature has its value. The only danger is lest we should make too much of it, and forget that God's Spirit has been working in the Church steadily until to-day, and opening to us fresh aspects of truth, which were hidden from the eyes of the early Christians. With regard to the whole question of High Church *versus* Low—I can only say that, to my mind, both parties represent great truths, on which, however, they are disposed to lay too much stress. I do not, for instance, care much whether the succession of bishops has or has not been unbroken from the earliest times. Episcopacy was not instituted by Jesus Christ. It was a convenient arrangement which was evolved out of the needs of the age—always, of course, under the direction of the Holy Spirit. The substantial continuity of the Christian Church is undisputed, and my view is that Christian ministers derive their authority from the Church of their own day. . . . . My advice to a young clergyman would be—flee controversy, as you would the Evil One. . . . . Systems are man-made things. ' Now we see as in a glass, darkly.' That is the truth. If any one says—' I can make everything plain,' believe him not. We know very little, very

little indeed. Think of all the volumes which have
been written about life beyond the grave. What are
they worth? What have they added to our knowledge?
Absolutely NOTHING " (Feb., 1886)

With regard, then, to Lefroy's religious opinions, I
think it may be concluded that Evangelicalism formed
the foundation, Anglicanism the superstructure, and
Latitudinarianism the coping-stone. But he cannot be
labelled as either a Low, High or Broad Churchman.
For the first, he was too much in sympathy with modern
thought; for the second, too spiritually self-centred :
and for the third, too definite in his convictions.

CHAPTER III

Nature never did betray
The heart that loved her.—WORDSWORTH.

Homo sum : humanum nihil a me alienum puto.
TERENCE.

THE year which immediately followed the warning of
the London physician was more fruitful in literary
production than any other period of Lefroy's life.
Possibly the consciousness of numbered days repressed
a certain fastidiousness in composition—or at least in
the publication of it—which was noticeable in his imma-
ture years. Except during intervals of great physical
prostration, we find him as energetic as ever in literary
and tutorial work, and lively correspondence with his
friends. We have before noted the sudden growth of
his social sympathies at Oxford. This sentiment was
never stronger than during the long years of his failing
health. It was the simple truth that he wrote to me
when the gloom was finally gathering round him : " I
think the story of my life is the story of its friendships.
Let it be written on my tombstone—*Dilexit multum.*"

It was not in Lefroy's nature to rest and rust. Being
strictly forbidden the excitement and strain of preaching
—no slight trial to a man of his gifts in the pulpit—he
took lodgings in Blackheath, and received private pupils.

The work was often elementary and exhausting, without
being lucrative. But not a few of those who came
under his care have expressed the deep debt they owe
to their contact with so pure and cultivated a mind.
During this period Lefroy was a loyal and active
supporter of his old school. He was a constant atten-
dant in all weathers at their football and cricket matches,
and he thus formed many friendships which largely
added to the happiness of his later years. He continued
to review for the *Guardian*. The particular section
assigned him was hardly that which he would have
chosen. He had to wade through tomes of second-rate
theological productions. He did his best to find in
most of them matter for eulogy, but we find him confessing to a friend his opinion that "the religious
reading public has a marvellous power of consuming
twaddle." He was a quick workman. He mentions
that one day a parcel of eighteen books arrived from the
Guardian office. "I reviewed several before the day
closed. They are all religious, and mostly devotional.
I do not know that there is one which I should have
bought. But I suppose *somebody* buys them. To my
mind, the best part of the whole lot is the binding of
half a dozen " (June, 1883).

The fact is that Lefroy's mind was of too refined and
delicate a texture for scholastic or journalistic drudgery.
Poets have occasionally made good journalists—when
allowed to choose their own topics—though I doubt
whether the pedagogic and poetic arts have any natural
points of affinity.

But Lefroy did not excuse himself from the effort of
original work, as many in his state of health might have
done, on the plea of preoccupation in these routine
duties. He produced and published in rapid succession
in 1883 four booklets of sonnets, " Echoes from Theo-

critus," "Cytisus and Galingale," "Windows of the Church," and "Sketches and Studies." Most of these subsequently appeared in one volume in 1885 under the title of "Echoes from Theocritus and other Sonnets" (Elliot Stock.) This volume being now out of print, its contents are included in the present edition.

The little book found its way by a happy chance to Mr. J. Addington Symonds at Davos in December, 1891 —a few months, alas! after Lefroy's death. For one cannot but regret that two men who at heart had so much in common, as Symonds instinctively felt (*cf.* p. 22), were not brought together in friendly correspondence. With his quick and generous appreciation of a kindred spirit (" for the book has only been in my hands a couple of hours "), Symonds wrote to me, " I feel sure already that here is the work of a poet born with a gift of wide compass in the line he chose to follow, and how sincere, direct, spontaneous, rich in fancy! It is so difficult to feel clear and sure about most books of the kind ; and so unutterably sad to think that the singer has already been taken from us " (Dec. 2, 1891). When I had supplied him with some account of Lefroy, especially with regard to his death, about which he had asked for particulars, Symonds wrote again, " The sonnets cannot die. They have the stuff of immortality, and will stir every generous soul to sympathy, if only they are not whelmed beneath the mass of late Victorian literature" (Dec. 11, 1891). The same letter contains an offer to write some study of Lefroy's work. This is now reproduced (*v.* Preface).

A few months later he writes, " I am deeply possessed with the desire to extend the influence which Lefroy's poems and ways of feeling ought to exert ; and I think I am right in saying that there exists a medium in our modern life which would be receptive of them, and for which they could not fail to be beneficial if once received. What I should like to do is to strengthen and expand the exposition I made in this first attempt, so as to present a more perfect view of Lefroy's mind from the side of his artistic and sympathetic qualities, and in particular, to discriminate the specific quality of his neo-Hellenism and to prevent any one from imagining that his athletic poems implied the least sympathy with licence. If one could only put quite rightly what he was in these matters, I am certain we should do something to draw some young souls of men and boys out of a Cretan labyrinth where lurks a minotaur." He also proposed "to make some excerpts from his address on Muscular Christianity, showing in what way he defined himself against the line taken in 1877 by myself and Pater" (March, 1892).

I deplore that, through the premature death of Symonds soon afterwards, this fuller appreciation was never executed, and that the "celata virtus" of Lefroy's genius must remain unsung by that "vates sacer," who by his artistic and intellectual sympathy was peculiarly fitted to erect a monument which might have been permanent. *Sunt lacrimæ rerum.*

The main lines, however, of what Symonds's fuller essay would have been, are clearly indicated in the appended article. To this estimate, so full of appreciation and critical sympathy, I shall attempt to add nothing, merely supplementing it by a few extracts from Lefroy's letters which refer to the composition of his sonnets.

In early days Lefroy had written lyrical verse in profusion, but, after his mind had matured, he rarely indulged in any but the sonnet form. One of his reasons is: "When one reads such flawless, such exquisite poetry as Austin Dobson's 'At the sign of the Lyre' or his 'Old World

Idylls,' one despairs of ever producing anything to match it. Nothing would induce me to put forth such stuff as ordinary verse-books are made of" (Nov., 1885). And another is: "I dare not write ordinary lyrics. Rhyming has become *too* easy. Only a sonnet, with its many assonances, seems to offer a task worthy of being overcome. . . . . Within the last year I have written between fifty and sixty sonnets, but I should have accomplished double that number if you had been similarly engaged." The friendly rivalry which Lefroy here invites in "provoking one another to good works" in the field of letters is a generous trait in his character, and sufficiently unusual in the *genus irritabile vatum* to deserve a passing notice. Some of the sonnets have a peculiar personal interest from the circumstances under which they were written. For example, "A Palaestral Study" (which Symonds rightly singles out as "very finely conceived and splendidly expressed") Lefroy sends to a friend with these words: "Enclosed is my last sonnet, poor enough for burning, but if you knew the horrors of the night-watch, during which it was born, you would bottle it in spirits as a pathological curiosity" (Feb., 1884).

Lefroy claims no particular originality for his thirty Theocritean sonnets. He confesses that "these very pagan compositions are not wholly satisfactory to my ecclesiastical (*sic*) mind. They were almost all written during the half-hour devoted to an after-dinner doze." He takes a modest view of his powers. "It is always risky for an inferior artist to attempt work which has absolutely no intrinsic value, but claims the right to exist wholly and solely on account of the perfection of its finish."* But strong as was Lefroy's passion for literary grace and finish, and still more for the models

* See the Sonnet, "A torchbearer."

of Hellenic poetry and sentiment which exhibited these qualities most perfectly, he was alive to the moral danger of a too unrestrained indulgence in the sensuous charms of classical literature. Here, as elsewhere, he shows his characteristic self-control.

> Sunt certi denique fines,
> Quos ultra citraque nequit consistere rectum.

Quoting the saying of F. W. Robertson, that there was a danger lest a man's artistic perception might, from the point of view of practical usefulness, be over-cultivated, he adds, "'Art for Art's sake' is not a good motto for the practical labourer. Even in poetry we ought to be Brownings, not Swinburnes. The moral purpose should never give place to the artistic design." The self-reproach which follows was hardly merited. "My pen has been allowed to write without a moral purpose. I have striven for an artistic excellence which I am not clever enough to attain. I have lost the satisfaction, which *might* have been mine, of helping, however slightly, the cause of noble activity." For, those who knew Lefroy personally as an unselfish and unwearied friend, cannot read his beautiful sonnet "The Poet," without recalling that he lived up to, as well as conceived, the true ideal. Indeed, his practical temperament revolted from a mere passive idealism: the reality and importance of actual life attracted him more than the fairest dreams of pre-Raphaelite fancy. Thus he writes: "Every fine figure, every bright face, every graceful movement abases me in the dust. I grovel while I worship. It is so *much* better to be a poem than to write one.* I exclaim to myself—"O wretched man! You can only describe in language which is and must be utterly inadequate, no matter

* Compare the Sonnet, "From any poet."

how skilfully used, the thing which these boys and these girls ARE " (May, 1883).

Was Lefroy ever in love ? I regret, for the sake of the curious in this matter, that I can find no direct evidence that he was. It is somewhat strange that in this one province, of all others, he should have departed from the guiding principle of his life, and preferred idealism to experience.* In a letter written on the eve of his Ordination (from which I have already quoted), he seems, in a half ascetic spirit accidental to him, to set aside finally the *Ars Amatoria* and all its works. But I do not think that the renunciation cost him much pain. Quoting in full Mr. Austin Dobson's graceful poem " Autonoë," he concludes : " I am not quite sure that Mr. Dobson has quite hit off the features of my ideal. Perhaps it inclines rather to be sex-less—serene beauty uncontaminated by a suspicion of fleshliness. But I know that it is Greek " (March, 1878).

Again : " In missing love and matrimony I have undoubtedly missed one (or should I rather say two ?) of life's good things. But considering the state of my health it is a merciful dispensation of Providence which has allowed me to find my happiness in dream-faces. . . . . Happily for myself, my admiration of beauty is purely a-sexual : and though I readily admit that the average of beauty is much higher (and the beauty itself lasts much longer) among girls than among boys ; yet here and there I could pick you out an Antinous, who, on purely artistic grounds, would bear away the palm from a Helen " (Dec., 1883).

Did space allow, I should be tempted to fill in by the help of Lefroy's letters the outline which Symonds has sketched, and to show that Lefroy's neo-Hellenism did

* I do not think that Lefroy's Lyrics on Love imply anything more than this.

not imply "the least sympathy with license" either in his athletic poems, or in his own personal character and conduct. The simple fact is that he had an instinctive admiration for all that was beautiful and graceful in human form and movement, into which he invariably tried to read a corresponding beauty of soul.* I think Lefroy misread his own character when he attributed this—as I think *instinctive*—love for the beautiful to a *deliberate* effort to externalise himself, to crush down morbid growths of an unsound body, and to " strive to enter into another man's—a healthier man's — consciousness, and to look at things as I found he looked at them." No doubt Lefroy attempted this in his general *external* demeanour in company, when he was suffering from great bodily weakness, but not, I think, in matters of art and physical or spiritual beauty. But he must be allowed to speak for himself. "This much I may say for myself—that my morbidity has in great part taken the shape of an excessive "—note that he admits the attribute—"admiration for what is *not* morbid. Only the other day I was walking to a football match with one of the players—a young fellow with every virtue under heaven, my superior alike in solid learning and simple faith, who plays a manly game as might the son of Alcmena, and smiles like the Hermes of Praxiteles—and I thought to myself 'If Olympus were extinguished to-morrow, I should still have a God.' It was a passing idiocy, of course ; and this particular kind of spasm afflicts me less than it used. But I think it proves that I reverence—though too wildly—what is not in itself unworthy of respect. Your Plato, at all events, would have excused me ! " (Nov., 1886).

Lefroy once remarked that athletics (as a spectacle)

---

* Compare the Sonnet " To E. C. P."
† Compare the Sonnet " To an invalid."

had made him a poet. Mr. Andrew Lang complimented him as the first sonneteer on football and cricket. To a friend who questions whether football is a fit subject for poetry Lefroy replies that "the human beings who play it may be so. . . . . When they 'line up' to catch the ball from touch "—Lefroy did not care for 'Association'—"and one gets a clear vision of the whole gang, snorting, palpitating with wild eyes and passionate mouths, one realises the magnificent beauty of young life as at no other time. . . . . My poetic soul gets an infusion of red blood whenever I am brought into contact with vigorous, energising humanity." And his enthusiasm for cricket was as keen. "There is something gracefully idyllic about the pastime. Given a bright day and a green sward, with a company of lithe young fellows scattered over it in picturesque attire—what could the artistic eye desire in addition? 'Earth has not anything more fair.' . . . . I play by proxy when I am able to watch the prowess of my luckier friends. *Floreal Cricket in æternum !* "

And again: "It *is* something to be able to play cricket well. . . . . The whole edifice of the Christian virtues could be raised on a basis of good cricket."

It has been remarked in the first chapter that Lefroy felt little interest in philosophy—at least in the form of metaphysical abstractions. Writing to a friend who did, he says: "I am glad you are going to take another dip into Plato. He is certainly my pet philosopher. He never gets far away from *man*. . . . . In my humble view an ounce of Plato is worth a pound of Kant or Fichte. It is ridiculous to see how men pride themselves on their power of 'abstract thought,' as they call it. There is no such thing as abstract thought. Why, you can't even conceive colour apart from some coloured thing. And yet these metaphysicians pretend to soar

into the infinite! . . . . Stick to *man*. Examine him,
dissect him, analyse him as much as you please. Read
Darwin and H. Spencer, and, if you have leisure,
take a medical degree. But don't 'soar'! Avoid
moonshine, though it be guaranteed 'A 1' double-
distilled by a German philosopher " (July, 1886).

He proceeds: "But all men are not so brutally materialistic as I am." And again, in a more serious vein, to the
same friend: "I envy you your taste for metaphysics.
I would give a great deal to share it. To an invalid,
before whose eyes death and eternity loom very large,
no more precious boon could be bestowed than a faith
in the power of the human intellect to grasp the unseen.
I don't of course for one moment question the *existence*
of the unseen, but it is hard for me to believe that Kant
or Comte, or any other mortal, can appreciate anything
except through the medium of their five bodily senses.*
And I don't see how physically-derived sensations can
possibly form a basis for supersensual ideas " (*cf.*
Mr. A. J. Balfour's argument in "The Foundations
of Belief"). But, in truth, I have probably spoilt
myself for the fine wheat-flour of metaphysics. I have
fed on oatmeal too long. I have found too abun-
dant satisfaction in the shapes of material beauty of
which the earth is full . . . . and 'worshipped the
creature more than the Creator' " (Feb., 1891).

Lefroy's ultra-practicalness comes out again in the
following: "There may be idealism, active idealism, in
art; but in politics, I think not. Did Bacon try to carry
out his political ideas? Did Hobbes influence the
statesmen of his time? Was Selden a power in the
world of 'affairs' as he was in the world of letters?
Take even Sir Thomas More. True, he died for his

---

* Compare the Sonnet, "An apology," especially the last
couplet.

principles, but is there any evidence that he actively attempted to realise ' Utopia ' ? Perhaps our latest idealist in politics was Disraeli. Do you think he allowed the favourite outline of his fancy to influence his actions, unless the expediency of the moment dictated an equivalent course ? " (July, 1886).

This is not the place to criticise these only half-serious utterances, or we might perhaps reply that there have been few *less* metaphysical philosophers than Comte, that few have soared more persistently than Plato into the impalpable empyrean of abstract thought (unless when compelled to earth to enforce the practical ethics of his master, Socrates), and that the proverbial " brutal materialism "—*not* idealism—of the philosopher of Malmesbury was, at any rate on its political side, a very concrete defence of a very concrete form of Absolutism, which no power, physical or philosophical, could long have bolstered up in the face of the stronger forces then gathering against it.

It may also be questioned whether Poetry, at least in her higher flights, is not at least as liable as " Divine Philosophy " to the charge of remoteness from the daily life and needs of man. But Lefroy would have been the last to maintain, or to wish that his own tastes and theories should always satisfy the demands of consistency, and we note in him (as perhaps in Walt Whitman) an incomplete fusion of materialistic and idealistic elements. But still, as Symonds truly observes, these " elements were kindlier mixed " in him than in most men.

Lefroy's letters and diaries abound in passing criticisms of the books he is reading. Literary style appealed most forcibly to his temperament, though the moral and intellectual aspect was rarely lost sight of. Tennyson, on the whole, was his favourite poet, yet

" Keats and Shelley have given me more *pleasure* than I
have ever gained from the Laureate.   Wordsworth and
Browning have each more deeply stimulated my *thought*.
and D. G. Rossetti in some of his sonnets simply thrills
my soul. . . . . Browning is certainly sometimes obscure.
but not so often as people make out.   And to express
subtle thoughts *simply* is impossible " (May, 1884).
" Bishop Blougram " was a special favourite with Lefroy.
Again, as to Rossetti : " In my opinion his sonnets are the
most masterly in the language.   There is no ' prettiness '
about them, but the power they contain is marvellous.
The eight years they spent underground in his wife's
coffin did not diminish their vitality " (Oct., 1882).

On estimates of Wordsworth Lefroy writes : " Mr.
Myers is an excellent guide to the student of Wordsworth, for he possesses both genius and sympathy.   It
is interesting to compare his monograph with Matthew
Arnold's Preface to the ' Golden Treasury ' selections,
which, clever as it may be, appears to lack altogether
the sense of fellowship necessary to the interpretation
of any poet worth the name."   But on Matthew
Arnold's own poetry : " How much beauty there is in
' Empedocles on Etna ' !   The opening scene is exquisite,
and all the songs of Callicles touch the true classic chord.
His account of the flaying of Marsyas has a peculiar
charm for me :

> ' Then Apollo's minister
> Hanged upon a branching fir
> Marsyas, that unhappy faun,
> And began to whet his knife.'

The passage opening thus, and ending, ' Poor Faun, ah,
poor Faun ' is a real gem.   I like it better than anything
in the ' Strayed Reveller,' though that too is a poem
steeped in Greek sentiment, and contains phrases

which no one but an Hellenic scholar could have originated."

And lastly on Jane Austen, who was the aunt of Lefroy's grandmother, on his father's side : " I hardly know which I admire most—her knowledge of the feminine heart, or the literary skill with which she puts it into words . . . . Looking at her own life-history, one can only marvel at the brilliancy and firmness of her touch, and the clever economy of social knowledge which enabled her to drape half a dozen stories with such a slender amount of material. . . . . What delights *me* is to find, as I do in her books, page after page of language so pointed, so balanced, so entirely perfect, that not the smallest word could be altered for the better. Such writing may be found in George Eliot's novels, but is exceedingly rare in the work of a woman. George Eliot probably owed her literary art to her study of the classics—the beauty of which is largely of the formal kind ; but Miss Austen's learning, so far as I know, did not extend to Greek, or even to Latin. So it is really a mystery whence she derived her power of exquisite workmanship; or perhaps I should say, not *power* (for care and patience will bring that), but the sense that such an ideal was worth striving after. Most women, even clever literary women, would be blind to the charm of it. To say so is no slur upon them. The fault is in their education. Their power of *general* artistic appreciation is certainly not deficient " (Diary, Dec., 1883).

If there is anything in Lefroy's last sentences, it will be interesting to observe how the growing study of the classics by women will affect the woman's novel of the future.

The publication of the "Sonnets" in 1885 brought Lefroy a large number of appreciative letters, which were very gratifying to him in the secluded life which his health compelled him to lead.

Christina Rossetti wrote : "To be told that something written by me has done good is a blessing indeed, and to know that it has given comfort adds the finishing grace. I have been enjoying your ' Sonnets ' to-day. . . . How rich in charm Theocritus must be, say I, to whom his words are inaccessible, but not yours. The sonnet on my dear brother's art touched me, and in some degree I see his work with your eyes." (Lefroy afterwards explained to Miss Rossetti that the sonnet on her brother did not profess to be an adequate estimate of his genius, being written a few hours after his first and only visit to the exhibition at Burlington House.)

Mr. Andrew Lang wrote : " I know few sonnets that give me so much pleasure as yours, in spite of my persistently ' Edinburgh ears ' " (cf. Lefroy's preface to the " Sonnets " on this criticism). " Your ' Sonnets from Theocritus ' are delightful, only (as a Scot) I do not like ' dawn ' rhyming to ' horn,' ' morn,' &c. Perhaps I over estimate the sonnets " (Mr. Lang is only speaking of the " Echoes from Theocritus," the rest not yet having been published) " because of their subject, but I like them better than any I have seen for long. As the public hates sonnets, I hope you will also write in other measures."

The late Archbishop of Canterbury wrote : " In days when there is so much careless, pretty writing and versifying, it is quite strengthening to see the real devotion to true work which the making of sonnets means. I have read many of your sonnets with pleasure, and feel sure that you will never yield to the ' extemporal ' *cacoethes.*" Referring to the two sonnets, " In the Cloisters, Winchester College," Dr. Benson continued : " We both feel that your lingering and musing

over a sod so dear to us in so sweet a place is even now
grateful to our hearts, and a tenderness to ourselves, as
well as an emotion of your own. God seemed to have
marked the boy to do great things here—and what he
is doing *there* is never far from our thoughts."

Similar letters—all of praise—came from Browning,
Lord Tennyson, Lord Leighton, Mr. Myers, Mr. Gosse,
and several others.

The year 1883—one of great physical prostration—
saw the production of a volume of sermons entitled,
" The Christian Ideal and other Sermons " (Skeffington
& Son, London). It embodies Lefroy's religious convictions, as the sonnets do his literary leanings—though
the two sides were rarely far apart in his nature. The
sermons do not deal with controversial questions or
intellectual difficulties ; they very rarely enter upon
doctrinal matter. On the other hand, they are not
merely moral essays. They disclose a pure and refined
soul, keenly alive to the importance and uncertain
tenure of life. They press home the paramount duty of
living and teaching others to live, *now* and *here*, by the
pattern of Christ. Practical idealism is their key-note.
The style is clear and incisive, the illustrations at once
poetical and homely, and the lessons plain and simple.

The Literary Churchman (Oct., 1883) well defines
their aim : " Mr. Lefroy does not address the rustic
or the highly educated, but that large central mass
of persons who, though unlearned, are yet thoroughly
capable of thought." In his preface he expressly
states that they were preached to " middle-class con-
gregations in a London suburb." Lefroy afterwards
heard that a lady in his congregation obliterated
these 'offensive' words from her copy of the book !
Commenting on this performance, which greatly
amused him, Lefroy writes, " I should have no hesi-

tation in describing my own humble personality by the 'offensive' term. What am I, unless 'middle-class'? As for being ashamed of it, why, I reckon the title the proudest an Englishman can bear. For unless I am much mistaken, it is the 'middle-class' which has made England what she is. *Floreat* Middle Class!"

A few passages selected from this volume of sermons will indicate wherein Lefroy held the Christian life to consist. "The man who has an object in life is an idealist. He sets up for himself an idea, a picture of the mind, as a goal, and he shapes the course of his actions towards that end. He does not dream. He does not romance. Once for all he registers his resolve. . . . . And the characteristic of his life is industry, effort and labour. And this ideal in religious terms bids us be perfect as God is perfect. We must try to be as perfect in *our* sphere as He is in His. Perfection has nothing to do with magnitude." * Lefroy's conscious-ness of the frail tenure of his own life lent a peculiar impressiveness to his enforcement of St. Paul's precept, 'As we have opportunity, let us do good unto all men.' "We must be so sensitive to the needs of other men, that, when they approach us, we instinctively attempt to do them good. It will require the experience of years, the habit of a lifetime, to make us swift and effectual ministers of good to our fellows. . . . . Good will and right purpose cannot at once bring swiftness and dexterity." And the humbleness of our sphere of beneficence need not dispirit us. "The glory of Christianity has always been that it does great things with *small* powers (or powers that men think small), and the results of its work remain. Don't say that you have no *power*. Look into your own bosom: find out

* See his Rondeau, "Heroism," and the Sonnet, "To a worker resigned."

what gives you pleasure, and then make it your business to give other men the like. Don't say that you have no *sphere*. Your world may be limited, but it is quite large enough for love. In fact, love cannot deal with communities, *as such*." 'Strength in weakness' was a favourite principle of Lefroy's. Reminding his hearers how even in the realm of letters Milton with his blindness, Pope with his crippled frame, Cowper with his melancholy, the consumptive Keats and the fragile Shelley were witnesses how the soul could triumph over the body, he concludes, "Perhaps the man who is helpful in most ways to his fellows is the man who combines weakness and strength in a varying proportion. . . . . St. Paul, I think, was such a man."

His reflections on the text 'We all do fade as a leaf' are instinct with poetical sensibility and a hope full of immortality built upon a basis of calm and clear-sighted reasoning. "We all do fade as a leaf. But as a leaf, we shall live again. Out of these dead leaves will be fashioned the bright young foliage of another May. By their death they are fertilising the soil from which the broad trunks draw strength and energy to sprout anew. . . . There is no loss of energy, no break in vital continuity. Death is only change, only the restful shadow between day and day. . . . We too shall live again in the generations which come after us. Having flourished our appointed time, we shall fall silently from the tree, and leave the branche clear for another and a younger race. And this race will be, under God, just what we, by our living and dying, have made them. . . . But we can rise higher than this; we may rise to a precious confidence in which the lesson of the leaves cannot help us. They will live again beyond all question, but only in a corporate and collective way. Not on every leaf as

it falls can we read ' Resurgam.'*. . . . But it is the
confidence in a particular resurrection, and this alone,
which lights the deathbed of the Christian, and dries
the tears of the mourners as they lay a brother in
the earth." It is true that these are, after all, only
common and familiar thoughts, but, viewed in the light
of Lefroy's life and death, they illustrate how completely
he moulded his character on the Christian ideal, and
how the Cross of Christ was for him a living and a
sustaining reality.

I have remarked before that Lefroy left behind him
at Oxford a certain controversial spirit which journalism, and possibly the *genius loci*, had for the time
developed. From that time he rarely indulged in
theological controversy, thinking it to be neither
helpful to the cause of truth, or to the practical
usefulness of the disputant. I know of only one
instance in which he departed from this rule. It is
worth quoting, as an illustration of Lefroy's view of
the relations of the doctrine of evolution to the
principles of morality. Dr. Stanley Leathes, in his
" Discourses on the Ten Commandments," had maintained that the moral law was not merely sanctioned
by, but that it originated in, the Decalogue. Lefroy
writes, " How these duties came to be regarded as
such the Bible does not tell us. We may believe, if
we please, that the consciousness of them was im-
planted by God, fully developed, in the mind of man
—that right notions about morality were originally
intuitive. Or, we may hold that the human conscience
has grown with the growth of the race, being quick-
ened and deepened by the action of society, through
many successive generations. . . . . I maintain that the

* See the Lyric, " Autumn leaves."

latter view is as Scriptural as the first. It harmonises quite as easily with the creed of the Saviour. . . . . We may reasonably bear with Mr. H. Spencer, while he investigates the history of moral ideas. He can discover nothing which we need fear to learn." * From other writings of Lefroy it is evident that he accepted without reserve Mr. Spencer's utilitarian and sociological theory of the origin of the moral sense, preferring it to the theory of an intuitive perception of right and wrong—on the principle of not needlessly multiplying miracles.

In 1885 Lefroy published his last book, "Counsels for the Common Life—six addresses to senior boys in a public school" (Skeffington & Son). Lefroy was at his best in these discourses. His thorough knowledge of, and sympathy with, the character, interests and ambitions of a school-boy, would have made him an inspiring head-master had his health allowed. Mr. Symonds was especially struck with the originality and power of the address on "Class-Making," and at his suggestion it is reprinted in this volume.

Six years of life still remained to Lefroy. Though his mind continued no less active, and his interest in the world, and especially in the successes of his friends, was in no way impaired by his constant sufferings, he was now unequal to any sustained productions in prose or in poetry. A few semi-scientific papers read to literary societies, and some occasional poems, are all that belong to this period.

* *The Family Churchman,* Dec. 27, 1883.

CHAPTER IV

THE END

First our pleasures die, and then
Our hopes, and then our fears, and when
These are dead, the debt is due,
Dust claims dust, and we die too.
                                SHELLEY.

Sleep after toil, port after stormy seas,
Ease after war, death after life, does greatly please.
                                SPENSER.

Θαρρῶ τῷ διοικοῦντι.
                                MARCUS AURELIUS.

WHEN Lefroy learned, in the summer of 1882, on the highest medical authority, that he was suffering from an incurable affection of the heart, with other complications, and that he could only look forward to a short tenure of life, the blow was for the time undoubtedly severe. It is probably a mistake to suppose that such a summons comes with less shock to chronic invalids than to men in the full vigour of life. The former have grown so used to respites that the final sentence takes them by surprise. But although much pain and prostration followed, the end was still far off.

Lefroy soon faced the situation with his wonted self-mastery. Of this crisis he writes later in the Diary: " Being a creature of flesh and blood, I cannot of course divest myself of the essential characteristics of flesh and blood, and the fear of death is one of these. But as far as my soul and intellect are concerned, I am free from the shade of nervous apprehension. It is certainly a solemn and an awful position which I occupy, but, as the solemnity is realised, the dread disappears. . . . . When the final breakdown happened, I was undeniably much disturbed. My self-consciousness was too acute for any vague hope that the evil might prove curable. . . . . I saw from the first the (physically) desperate nature of my case. And I was frightened. But God dealt very gently with me. He did not call me from earth in a peremptory manner. He gave me time—ample time—to recover my faith, and taught me to trust Him as I had not trusted Him before. A year and a half is a long period. If a man cannot prepare for his great change in a year and a half, he could not so prepare in a hundred years. . . . . I shall die, as I have lived, a steadfast believer in the Cross of Christ; I shall die, as, alas! I have not always lived, an unfaltering disciple of the Risen Lord" (Nov., 1883).

About this time, visiting the grave of one of his athletic heroes who had been killed by a fall from his horse in the flower of his youth, Lefroy soliloquises thus: "It was Wordsworth who said that a grave is a very 'tranquillising' object, and no truer remark has ever been uttered. When I am nervous, anxious or depressed, a visit to a churchyard or a cemetery always soothes, and in a sense cheers me. 'After life's fitful fever he sleeps well'—that is the dominant idea which the sight of a grave invariably suggests. . . . . Life, thank God, is not necessarily a 'fitful fever' when regarded by itself, but by comparison with the slumber of a dead body it appears highly 'fitful and feverish,' even if lived under circumstances the most serene. After the calmest, happiest career, it is no forcing of language to say that a man 'sleeps well.' And (in my

own experience) the mere contemplation of this 'sleep'
is very restful to human thought and human care.
I am moved to write these words, because some
apologia seems needful to explain or excuse my
frequent 'meditations among the tombs.' I do not
think they are evidence of a morbid temperament. I
am sure they do not proceed from any want of sympathy with the living, breathing, sentient crowd, for I
still have the keenest appreciation of life in all its
forms. But death is the complement of life, and I find
it helpful, and it is (I hope) not unhealthy to recognise
that too " (Sept., 1883).

It must not be inferred from these extracts that
Lefroy's mind, even in these darkest days, was
absorbed in thoughts of self, sadness, or death. Indeed, the year 1883 was, as before stated, fuller than
any other of literary activity. It saw his sonnets and
sermons through the press. The Diary is full of the
details of publication, and his keen pleasure at their
favourable reception. His interest in the doings of his
friends continued unabated. *Nihil humani* was never
far from him. When somewhat convalescent he play-
fully rallies an old friend : "You must not cook your
correspondence to suit my supposed serious tastes.
Sober folk rather *prefer* to read of rollicking adventures
and Bohemian episodes because they have no personal
experience of them. Sometimes * * * * reads me your
letters to *him*, and I wonder whether his correspondent
is the same * * * * * who sends me new ideas about
the regeneration of society. Of course I don't want you
to forget that I am a Christian man and a clergyman,
but you may ocasionally, if you please, tell me something of the lighter side of your life—mine is dreary
enough " (Feb., 1884).

Again, to the same friend : " Life goes most uneventfully with me. Apart from the pressure of ill-health, there is not much in my days to remind me that I 'live' at all. The old time of activity is now so very far away that I am almost beginning to forget what activity means. It is difficult, for instance, to realise the life which you are now leading, so full of usefulness, so full of human interests " (March, 1885).*

But, though Lefroy was now debarred from active service in the world, he retained in a peculiar degree 'the human heart by which we live'—and die : " Life and not death is my heart's desire. Life and not death is the keynote of my conduct. As long as I live, I shall strive to take a full and healthy interest in all that pertains to life. My fellow men are still dear to me. The affairs of my friends are still near my heart. . . . . I like to feel that, though I am weak, others are strong. . . . It makes my own exit less important—if indeed the exit of any individual can be said to have importance. I leave no task unaccomplished which will not be easily and ably carried through by some one else. Perhaps I may even hope that my death will (for a while at least) stimulate my friends to keener efforts in the various good causes which have given us common interests "—here follow the names of his closest friends. " The members of my own family are not to be spoken of here. There is something sacred about the ties which bind brother and sister, parent and child. To discuss it is almost to profane it. Home has always been to me what I wish it were to every man—the brightest spot upon earth. I have never left it without sadness, or returned to it without joy. I count myself ' felix opportunitate mortis ' in that I die before the home of my childhood has lost one of its charms. God grant that they may long remain a blessing to

* Compare the Sonnet, " From a quiet place."

E

those whom I shall leave behind me!" (Diary, Nov.,
1883).

A regret which often came upon him at this period
that he "would not be able to watch the after-career of
many bright lads in whom I take an interest" leads
Lefroy on to a reflexion, in which the Christian hope
soars above all limits of scientific speculation : "Perhaps
I have no right to assume this inability, seeing how
little is known of the powers of disembodied spirits.
Aristotle maintains this particular point in the 'Ethics,'
and discusses the probability of departed souls having
some knowledge of terrestrial affairs. He thinks that
such knowledge would detract from their perfect
felicity. Perhaps so; and yet in the presence of God
all seeming evils must be recognised as non-evils. Darkness can never be distressing to one who actually *sees*
the light beyond. Only a reflection of the world's pain
could make pain in heaven, and, where a thousand
years are as one day, there would be no time for such a
reflexion to impress itself separately from the reflexion
(or rather the real presence) of the ultimate bliss"
(August, 1883).

There were two biographies from which Lefroy drew
much comfort in his hours of weakness—that of Mrs.
Prentiss and that of F. W. Robertson. Of the former
he writes : "The book is largely made up of letters.
These are almost all *to* women, and were obviously
written *by* a woman. In fact, Mrs. Prentiss with all
her ability and strong sense had from first to last very
few masculine sympathies. . . . . Still I have found it
very pleasant, and I should be inclined to question the
spiritual sympathy of any man who differed from me. I
never before realised how nearly a commonplace career
may rise to the level of heroism, when all its multi-
farious and petty duties, relationships and opportunities

are dealt with in the noblest possible temper" (Diary, Sept., 1883).

And of the 'Life of F. W. Robertson': "The final scenes of that noble career have a deeper meaning for me than they had when I last thought about them. I can understand that 'prostration too dreadful to describe.' I can enter into the spirit of that cry, 'My God! My Father! My God! My Father!' I seem to hear those unutterably pathetic 'last words'—'Let me rest. I must die. Let God do His work'—spoken a few minutes before he passed away. It is perhaps a small matter that a dying man should retain consciousness to the last. Many people would not desire it, and some diseases do not permit of it. But when it happens to a hero of Robertson's stamp, it seems to give an added glory. The soul is triumphant over the body, and the triumph is visible to all around" (Diary, Nov., 1883).

When the end was, as Lefroy thought, at last come, he writes: "The shadow deepens, but not the gloom. 'Dominus illuminatio mea.' My spirit is wonderfully strengthened and sustained. Come what may, God will enable me to bear it. I feel beneath me the everlasting arms" (Diary, Nov., 1883).

Then follow rapid alternations of prostration and revival. A football match would always tempt him forth, although exhaustion nearly always succeeded the effort. The reviews for the *Guardian* were written with the old precision, and the congratulatory letters on his "Sonnets" were punctually answered. "Live while you live," was a maxim which Lefroy resolutely obeyed to the end.

The close of the year 1883 finds him "very far indeed from being out of danger, but in less bodily distress, thank God. . . . . O, for a glimpse of the sky!"

The entry on the last day of the year, when he practically ceased to keep a diary, is :

Φόβος οὐκ ἔστιν ἐν τῇ ἀγάπῃ, ἀλλ᾽ ἡ τελεία ἀγάπη ἔξω βάλλει τὸν φόβον, ὅτι ὁ φόβος κόλασιν ἔχει· ὁ δὲ φοβούμενος οὐ τετελείωται ἐν τῇ ἀγάπῃ.—S. John, ep. i. chap. iv. 18.

If this were not the record of an actual life, the narrative would close here. Lefroy had, in a sense, lived his life. But some years of bodily restfulness still remained. He resumed the daily round of duties, again took pupils, and again corresponded with his old friends. And indeed at times he seemed so wonderfully to regain his old vitality that we almost predicted for him a fresh career of usefulness in the Church, and of literary fertility. But the end was only delayed for a time. He had been granted, as he gratefully confessed, a respite during which to prepare for the great change. And he had employed it well. Truly of him it may be said, " Nothing in his life became him like the leaving of it."

When I saw him for the last time, he had been suffering much pain, but, though in great prostration of body, his mind was perfectly calm and clear. It was not all sadness to reflect that he had been spared the supreme trial which he had so often dreaded—the gradual failing of his mental powers, and had been granted the last and unspeakable solaces of love in that home which had always been to him "the brightest spot upon earth." In such tender keeping he passed away on the morning of September the 19th, 1891, 'after a night of intense suffering, patiently borne to the end.' He was laid to rest, by his own wish, in that Charlton Cemetery whither he had so often withdrawn to meditate upon "the sleep which is very restful to human thought and human care." Among the mourners, not least numerous were those young men and boys whose hearts he had won, and whose characters he had helped to mould by his pure example and unwearying sympathy.

> Life ! I know not what thou art,
> But know that thou and I must part :
> And when, or how, or where we met
> I own to me's a secret yet.
>
> Life ! we've been long together
> Through pleasant and through cloudy weather ;
> 'Tis hard to part when friends are dear—
> Perhaps 'twill cost a sigh, a tear.
>
> Then steal away, give little warning,
> Choose thine own time ;
> Say not Good Night, but, in some brighter clime,
> Bid me Good Morning.

ECHOES FROM THEOCRITUS

AND OTHER SONNETS

We live by admiration, hope, and love.
                              WORDSWORTH.

PREFACE

THE sonnets which compose this volume have, with one or two exceptions, already seen the light in the shape of pamphlets locally printed. The kind reception given to these has induced me to offer part of their contents to a larger public. May one be so bold as to disagree with Horace in his famous remark* about mediocrity in the poetic field, and without claiming for these verses any high degree of excellence, yet venture to hope that they may while away a vacant hour as legitimately and effectively as a second-rate biography or average novel?

A few special acknowledgments are necessary. In the "Echoes from Theocritus," it is Bishop Wordsworth's edition of the poet to which reference is made; but I am greatly indebted to Mr. Andrew Lang's excellent prose translation for renderings of particular words and phrases which very likely I should not have lighted upon without his aid. It will be noticed that the first five sonnets have no "text" in the Author. The rest are founded upon some one passage in the Idyls or Epigrams. How slight the foundation often is may be ascertained by any one curious enough to follow up the references given.

> * Mediocribus esse poetis
> Non homines, non di, non concessere columnæ.
> *De Arte Poëtica,* 372-3.

The influence of Mr. F. W. H. Myers's deeply interesting "Classical Essays" will be traced in the sonnets on "Virgil" and "Something Lost."

Sonnet LXVIII. is due in part to a lyric by Théophile Gautier, called "L'Art."

Judging from press-notices and private letters, I seem to have laid myself open to criticism in my use of rhymes. Will it be a fair reply to say that I am a Londoner born and bred, and therefore adopt the standard of pronunciation (doubtless very corrupt) which prevails among my fellow-citizens? In Edinburgh it is easy to believe that "dawn" does not rhyme with "morn." But London ears are less discriminating, and to London ears I appeal.

A final word of gratitude is due to my friend Mr. W. A. Gill, for the kind interest he has taken in these verses and the literary help he has bestowed upon them.

E. C. L.

42 SHOOTER'S HILL ROAD, S.E.

ECHOES FROM THEOCRITUS

BATTUS

O SUN-BROWNED shepherd, whose untutored grace
Awoke the singer of that southern isle,
What time he lingered in his father's place,
And bore not yet his music to the Nile :
How soon we make in life a tranquil space
Whenas, our foolish cares forgot the while,
We read the legend of thy classic face,
And catch the lustre of thy lyric smile.
Sing to us still in songs of tourney-type,
As if the jealous Milon loitered near,
Or let thy fingers twinkle o'er the pipe,
And breathe a mellow cadence sweet and clear,
Till all thy browsing lambs forego the ripe
Arbutus buds, and circle round to hear.

II

A SHEPHERD MAIDEN

ON shores of Sicily a shape of Greece !
Dear maid, what means this lonely communing
With winds and waves ?   What fancy, what caprice,
Has drawn thee from thy fellows ?   Do they fling
Rude jests at thee ?   Or seekest thou surcease
Of drowsy toil in noonday shepherding ?
Enough : our questions cannot break thy peace ;
Thou art a shade,—a long-entombèd thing.
But still we see thy sun-lit face, O sweet,
Shining eternal where it shone of yore ;
Still comes a vision of blue-veinèd feet
That stand for ever on a pebbly shore ;
While round, the tidal waters flow and fleet
And ripple, ripple, ripple, evermore.

III

DAPHNIS

WHEN Daphnis comes adown the purple steep
From out the rolling mists that wrap the dawn,
Leaving aloft his crag-encradled sheep,
Leaving the snares that vex the dappled fawn,
He gives the signal for the flight of sleep,
And hurls a windy blast from hunter's horn
At rose-hung lattices, whence maidens peep
To glimpse the young glad herald of the morn.
Then haply one will rise and bid him take
A brimming draught of new-drawn milk a-foam ;
But fleet his feet and fain ; he will not break
His patient fast at any place but home,
Where his fond mother waits him with a cake
And lucent honey dripping from the comb.

IV

A SICILIAN NIGHT

COME, stand we here within this cactus-brake,
And let the leafy tangle cloak us round.
It is the spot whereof the Seer spake—
To nymph and faun a nightly trysting-ground.
How still the scene ! No zephyr stirs to shake
The listening air. The trees are slumber-bound
In soft repose. There's not a bird awake
To witch the silence with a silver sound.
Now haply shall the vision trance our eyes,
By heedless mortals all too rarely scanned,
Of mystic maidens in immortal guise,
Who mingle shadowy hand with shadowy hand,
And moving o'er the lilies circle-wise,
Beat out with naked feet a saraband.

v

A SUMMER DAY IN OLD SICILY

Gods, what a sun ! I think the world's aglow.
This garment irks me. Phœbus, it is hot !
'T were sad if Glycera should find me shot
By flame-tipped arrows from the Archer's bow.
Perchance he envies me,—the villain ! O
For one tree's shadow or a cliff-side grot !
Where shall I shelter that he slay me not ?
In what cool air or element ? I know.
The sea shall save me from the sweltering land.
Far out I'll wade, till creeping up and up,
The cold green water quenches every limb.
Then to the jealous god with lifted hand
I'll pour libation from a rosy cup,
And leap, and dive, and see the tunnies swim.

VI

SIMAETHA, I

Idyl ii.

Go pluck me laurel-leaves, dear Thestylis,
From any bough that shimmers in the moon ;
To dread Selene pray the while, and miss
No single word of all the magic rune.
She, only she, can grant the lover's boon,
She, only she, restore a maiden's bliss ;
He comes not now, my sweet, but soon, O soon,
He will be waiting, watching, for my kiss
Twelve days ; ah ! is it twelve, since last we met ?
Quick wind about the bowl the ruddy skein !
He has forgotten : cruel to forget !
But this red wool shall rouse him into pain,
This charm of charms shall wake his passion yet.
O good my goddess, bring my Love again !

VII

SIMAETHA, II

Now take the barley grains, sweet Thestylis,
And fling them right and left upon the floor;
If still he lingers, Delphis' bones like this
Shall be disjoined upon a wreck-strewn shore.
See how I burn the laurel shoots. They hiss
And curl and crackle, blasted to the core;
And Delphis' flesh shall wither up like this
Unless he quickly seeks my shamèd door.
In brazen pans the wax is melting fast:
O gracious goddess, bid thy work begin!
So melt young Delphis, till he speeds at last,
Beneath my window wails his bitter sin,—
Begs me to pardon all his folly past
And of my clemency to let him in.

VIII

THE GOATHERD IN LOVE

Idyl iii. 1–7.

Good Tityrus, attend these goats awhile,
And let me seek where Amaryllis hides,
Crannied, I guess, beneath that rocky pile
With fern atop and ivy-mantled sides.
'Tis there most days the merry girl abides,
And flashes from her cave a sudden smile,
Which like a pharos-flame her lover guides
And makes him hope he looks not wholly vile.
If thou canst guard the flock while I am gone,
I will but notice how my lady fares,
Then hasten back and take the crook anon.
The goats are tame—the least of all my cares,
Save one, that tawny thief; keep watch upon
His bearing, lest he butt thee unawares.

IX

THE LOVE-SPELL

Idyl iii. 28–30.

I THOUGHT upon my lady as I strode
Last night from labour, and bemoaned my lot,
Uncertain if she loves or loves me not,
Who gives no sign or token; till the road
Bent round and took me past my Love's abode.
And then some happy chance, I know not what,
Moved me to try a spell long time forgot,
By which love's issue may be clear foreshowed.
I plucked a poppy from the wayside grass
And struck it sharply on my naked arm,
Striving to burst its inner heart. Alas!
The petals only clung in painless calm.
And then I knew how this could never be,
That my dear Love's dear heart should break for me.

X

SIMICHIDAS

Idyl vii. 21–26.

SIMICHIDAS, thou love-demented loon!
What haste is this, when no man's need doth call?
Surely the gods have witched thee. 'Tis high noon.
No creature else hath any strength at all;
The spotted lizard sleeps upon the wall;
The skiey larks drop earthward for the boon
Of one still hour; the ants forget to crawl.
Naught stirs except the stones beneath thy shoon.
Nay, but I know; not love impels thee thus;
Thy journey's end will bring a baser gain.
Some burgher's feast or vintner's overplus
Of trodden grapes—for these thy feet are fain.
Well, go thy way; be fortunate. But us
This pleasant shade retains and shall retain.

F

XI

AGEANAX

Idyl vii. 52–62.

Dear voyager, a lucky star be thine,
To Mytilenè sailing over sea,
Or foul or fair the constellations shine,
Or east or west the wind-blown billows flee.
May halcyon-birds that hover o'er the brine
Diffuse abroad their own tranquillity,
Till ocean stretches stilly as the wine
In this deep cup which now we drain to thee.
From lip to lip the merry circle through
We pass the tankard and repeat thy name;
And having pledged thee once, we pledge anew,
Lest in thy friends' neglect thou suffer shame.
God-speed to ship, good health to pious crew,
Peace by the way, and port of noble fame !

XII

COMATAS

Idyl vii. 78–82.

In the great cedar chest for one whole year
The pious goatherd by his lord confined,
Because he reckoned not his flock more dear
Than the dear Muse he served with loyal mind,
Was fed by ministers whom none can bind—
The blunt-faced bees that came from far and near,
Spreading the Muse's signal on the wind,
And found a crevice, and distilled the clear
Sweet juice of flowers to feed the prisoned thrall,
Till the slow months went round and he was free.
Then, tuneful herds, spare not the fold and stall
For sacrifice, nor fear your lord may see ;
The Muse can save her servants when they call—
The Muse who sped that long captivity.

XIII

AT THE SHRINE OF PAN

Idyl vii. 106–108.

O GOATISH god, I pray you ! Grant my prayer,
And in my view great Zeus is less divine :
Reject it,—at your peril,—if you dare !
And look no more for any gift of mine.
And who will then support this paltry shrine ?
Though you yourself subsist on frugal fare,
Others have wants, and as the wise opine,
'Tis never well to leave the cupboard bare.
Few thieves will quite good-humouredly forego
Their wonted booty from the sacred sod ;
And herb-whips sting ; I think at least you know
With what effect some boys can wield the rod.
Observe in time how thick these nettles grow,
And flee the shame that waits a pauper god.

XIV

AT THE FARM OF PHRASIDAMUS

Idyl vii. 133–146.

WHERE elm and poplar branch to branch have grown,
In cool deep shade the shepherds take their rest
On beds of fragrant vine-leaves newly strown,
Till the great sun declineth in the west.
From thorny thickets round, as if opprest
By secret care, the ring-dove maketh moan ;
With sudden cry from some remoter nest
The nooning owlet hunts in dreams alone ;
A merry noise the burnt cicalas make,
While honeyed horns are droning everywhere ;
The fruit-trees bend as though foredoomed to break
With burden heavier than their strength can bear,
And if the faintest zephyr seem to shake,
Drop down an apple now, and now a pear.

XV

THE SINGING-MATCH, I

Idyl viii.

FROM upland pastures, where the flocks are wending
Slow-footed ways through heather-bells and fern,
Comes down a sound with sea-born murmurs blending
Of lips that make sweet melody in turn.
'Tis Daphnis with Menalcas sharp-contending
For the bright flute which both are keen to earn;
While hard at hand a goatherd tarries, bending
Rapt ears of judgment while the singers burn.
Menalcas, first, hymns Love and all the blessing
Which haps to field and fold where Love's feet stray;
He tells of dearth and leanness clear confessing
What ills befall, should Love despised betray;
Ah, poor the man, though land and gold possessing,
In whose demesne no Love consents to stay.

XVI

THE SINGING-MATCH, II

THEN Daphnis strikes the note of one that plaineth,
Whose Love is not the Love he hoped to find;
A Love which after blandishment disdaineth
To bless the heart too readily resigned.
Slight snares indeed are they which Eros feigneth,
For well he knows that lover's eyes are blind,
But none the captured beast more keenly paineth
Than Love's entrapment cruelly unkind.
All things have grief at times.   When high winds
      shake it,
The grove is grieved with plaintive murmurings;
So grieves the woodland bird when fowlers take it,
To feel the net encompassing its wings;
And so the heart when peace and joy forsake it
At Love's enravishment.   Thus Daphnis sings.

XVII

THE SINGING-MATCH, III

AND last the goatherd, like as one awoken
From sylvan slumbers on a summer day,
Whose sleep is filled with birds, and only broken
Because the thrushes all have flown away,—
Uplifts his head, and with a word soft-spoken
Declares the victor in the bloodless fray:
" Thine is the flute, O Daphnis! Take the token,
For thou hast conquered with the crowning lay.
And, O, if thou wilt teach to carol brightly
This mouth of mine, as through the fields we go,
To thee shall fall a monster goat that nightly
Makes every milking-bowl to overflow."
Then clapped the lad his hands, and leapt as lightly
As weanling fawns that leap around the doe.

MENALCAS

Idyl viii. 63–66.

WITH limbs out-stretched along the thymy ground
The dog Lampûrus slumbers in the shade,
While tender ewes unchecked by warning sound
Go wandering idly through the sylvan glade,
In guileless ignorance all undismayed
By cruel beasts that hold the copse around
And make the herd Menalcas half-afraid—
The boyish herd who cries : " O heedless hound,
Is this thy helping of my timorous youth—
To let the flock disperse the woods among,
With no preventing feet, no faithful tongue?
The very wolves might show a deeper ruth,
And spare to raven with ensanguined tooth,
Seeing the shepherd of the sheep is young."

XIX

THE TOMB OF DIOCLES

Idyl xii. 27–33.

HERE, stranger, pause, and take a moment's ease
With pleasant thinking on a good man dead.
This marble marks the tomb of Diocles ;
Say not that virtue sleeps unhallowèd!
The grateful tribes delight with arts like these
To deck the pillow of a noble head.
Nor are these all ; beneath yon arching trees
The merriest chorus of the spring is led.
For on a day from country cots around
Come troops of ruddy children fair of face,
And forming rings about this holy ground,
Contest the guerdon of a bright embrace ;
And whoso kisseth with the deftest grace
Goes homeward to his mother, happy, crowned.

XX

HYLAS

Idyl xiii.

WHAT pool is this by galingale surrounded,
With parsley and tall iris overgrown ?
It is the pool whose wayward nymphs confounded
The quest of Heracles to glut their own
Desire of love.   Its depths hath no man sounded
Save the young Mysian argonaut alone,
When round his drooping neck he felt, astounded,
The cruel grasp that sank him like a stone.
Through all the land the Hero wandered, crying
" Hylas !" and " Hylas !" till the close of day,
And thrice there came a feeble voice replying
From watery caverns where the prisoner lay ;
Yet to his ear it seemed but as the sighing
Of zephyrs through the forest far away.

XXI

THE TUNNY-FISHERS

Idyl xxi.

In rude log-cabin by the lone sea-shore
Two aged fishers slept the sleep of toil.
Rough was their life, and scant their household store,
Scarce aught but hooks and nets and seamen's coil.
To one of these came visions of strange spoil ;
He caught a fish—such fish as none before
Caught ever, bright with sheen and glittering foil,
A golden fish ; and made high vows no more
To sail the seas, but spend the troven gold ;
Then woke and wept to starve or be forsworn.
To whom his fellow : "Surely, being old,
Thou drivellest. Vow and vision both are born
Of air. Catch living fish or die." And cold
Through eastern windows crept the ashy dawn.

XXII

THE YOUTH OF HERACLES

Idyl xxiv. 101-102.

As when in flowerful gardens, lofty-girt
With thicket-hedge of ilex, oak, and vine,
Where northern breezes do no mortal hurt,
And warmer suns have constant leave to shine,
A tender sapling, be it larch or pine,
Shoots always upwards with a daily spirt,
Thanks to the woven boughs that round it twine,
Thanks to the shelter of its leafy skirt :
So in a tranquil and secluded place,
Where never pierced the faintest note of harm,
The Argive hero grew and waxed apace,
Enclosed and compassed by Alcmena's arm ;
And knew not as he watched the mother's-face
The mother's-love that fenced him from alarm.

XXIII

THE FLUTE OF DAPHNIS

Epigram ii.

I am the flute of Daphnis.   On this wall
He nailed his tribute to the great god Pan,
What time he grew from boyhood, shapely, tall,
And felt the first deep ardours of a man.
Through adult veins more swift the song-tide ran,—
A vernal stream whose swollen torrents call
For instant ease in utterance.   Then began
That course of triumph reverenced by all.
Him the gods loved, and more than other men
Blessed with the flower of beauty, and endowed
His soul of music with the strength of ten.
Now on a festal day I see the crowd
Look fondly at my resting-place, and when
I think whose lips have pressed me, I am proud.

XXIV

A SACRED GROVE

Epigram iv.

I know a spot where love delights to dream,
Because he finds his fancies happen true.
Within its fence no myrtle ever grew
That failed in wealth of flower ; no sunny beam
Has used its vantage vainly.   You might deem
Yourself a happy plant and blossom too,
Or be a bird and sing as thrushes do,
So sweet in that fair place doth nature seem.
A matted vine invests the rocks above,
And tries to kiss a runlet leaping through
With endless laughter.   Hither at noon comes Love
And woos the god who is not hard to woo,
Taking his answer from the nested dove
That ever hymneth skies for ever blue.

XXV

A SYLVAN REVEL

Epigram v.

WHAT ho! my shepherds, sweet it were
To fill with song this leafy glade.
Bring harp and flute.   The gods have made
An hour for music.   Daphnis there
Shall give the note a jocund blare
From out his horn.   The rest will aid
Wiih fifes and drums, and charm the shade,
And rout the dusky wings of care.
We'll pipe to fox and wolf and bear.
We'll wake the wood with rataplan,
Fetch every beast from every lair,
Make every creature dance who can,
Set every Satyr's hoof in air,
And tickle both the feet of Pan!

XXVI

THYRSIS

Epigram vi.

SAD Thyrsis weeps till his blue eyes are dim,
Because the wolf has torn his pride away,—
The little kid so apt for sport and play,
Which knew his voice and loved to follow him.
Who would not weep that cruel fate and grim
Should end her pranks on this unhappy day,
And give her tender innocence a prey
For savage jaws to harry limb from limb?
Yet think, O shepherd, how thy tears are vain
To rouse the dead or bring the slain again;
Beyond all hope her body lies, alack!
Devoured she is; no bones of her remain.
The leaping hounds are on the murderer's track,
But will they, can they, bear thy darling back?

XXVII

CLEONICUS

Epigram ix.

LET sailors watch the waning Pleiades,
And keep the shore. This man, made over-bold
By godless pride, and too much greed of gold,
Setting his gains before his health and ease,
Ran up his sails to catch the whistling breeze :
Whose corpse, ere now, the restless waves have rolled
From deep to deep, while all his freight, unsold,
Is tossed upon the tumult of the seas.
Such fate had one whose avaricious eyes
Lured him to peril in a mad emprise.
Yea, from the Syrian coast to Thasos bound,
He slipped his anchor with rich merchandise,
While the wet stars were slipping from the skies,
And with the drowning stars untimely drowned.

XXVIII

THE EPITAPH OF EUSTHENES

Epigram xi.

A BARD is buried here, not strong, but sweet ;
A Teacher too, not great, but gently wise ;
This modest stone (the burghers thought it meet)
May tell the world where so much virtue lies.
His happy skill it was in mart and street
To scan men's faces with a true surmise,
Follow the spirit to its inmost seat,
And read the soul reflected in the eyes.
No part had he in catholic renown,
Which none but god-inspirèd poets share ;
Not his to trail the philosophic gown,
That only sages of the School may wear ;
But his at least to fill an alien town
With friends, who make his tomb their loving care.

XXIX

THE MONUMENT OF CLEITA

Epigram xviii.

HERE Cleita sleeps.   You ask her life and race ?
Read on, and learn a simple tale and true.
A nurse she was from the far land of Thrace,
Who tended little Medëus while he grew
A healthy, happy child, and did imbue
His nascent mind with godliness and grace ;
So fencing him from evil that he knew
No word of what is impious or base.
And when at length, her tale of years all told,
She came to lie in this reposeful spot,
Young Medëus, still a child, but sagely old,
Upreared this monument, that unforgot
The care beyond his recompense of gold
Might live a memory and perish not.

XXX

THE GRAVE OF HIPPONAX

Epigram xxi.

HERE lies a bard, Hippónax—honoured name !
Sweet were the songs that won him endless praise,
And yet his life was sweeter than his lays.
Traveller, a question fronts thee : Canst thou claim
Kinship with such in conduct void of blame ?
If not, forbear this precinct ; go thy ways ;
Lest some bright watcher of the tomb should raise
A jealous hand to cover thee with shame.
But if thy soul is free from shade of guilt,
Or, having sinned, hath been at length forgiven,
To thee all rights of common kin belong ;
Lay down thy weary limbs, and, if thou wilt,
Let slumber wrap them round, nor fear that Heaven
Will suffer any sprite to do thee wrong.

MISCELLANEOUS SONNETS

TO CERTAIN KIND CRITICS

O STALWART friends, O strong-souled flatterers,
Who bid me shape my verse in ampler mode,
And trumpet forth a ballad, epic, ode,—
How shall I answer you ? When impulse stirs
The genuine Bard, he soars unasked : but, sirs,
What power can lift the meaner sort ? Why goad
My ambling Muse along an upland road
Which leadeth not to any haunt of hers ?
She hath no mind for " freaks upon the fells,"
No wish to hear the storm-wind rattling by ;
She loves her cowslips more than immortelles,
Her garden-closes than the abysmal sky :
In a green dale her chosen sweetheart dwells :
The mountain-height she must not, dare not, try.

A WOODLAND STREAM, I

DRAWN by the noise of water, and its gleam
Flashed through the foxgloves nodding o'er the brink,
I lead my wayward fancy down to drink
From the still depths of this embow'red stream.
Arch over arch the sun-gilt branches link
Their shadowy leaves, escaped by many a beam
Cleaving the limpid wave, as sleepers sink
Through endless æther in a June-night dream.
Deep down in tranquil gloom, where happy breeds
A world of elfin shapes to light denied,
Amid lush tangle of the swaling weeds
The creatures of the streamlet leap and glide,—
Glad in the shelter of its tufted reeds,
Lulled by the ceaseless ripple of its tide.

III

A WOODLAND STREAM, II

How in this nook the ancient creed comes near,
And seems to keep its right untarnished still !
If there be guardian sprites of wood and rill,
I think a simple faith would see them here ;
A faith that watched the darkly rolling year
Through days of death and sleeping-times, until
The constant months their slow sad round fulfil
To wake the spring-god from his wintry bier.
Adonis !   Ah, it is not all profane—
This modern earth.   Come forth, ye choral band !
Your Lady bends to kiss the lips again,
The opening lips.   'Tis meet ye were at hand.
So ran the song through April wind and rain ;
And, lo, the glad fruition where I stand !

IV

A WOODLAND STREAM, III

I cannot tell what spirit-forms are free
To suck the secret of this green delight :
I only feel it was not made for *me*—
Not mine to use it with a spirit's right.
I am as other men—poor aliens we
From Nature's paradise in Heaven's despite,
Who only glimpse its charm with blinded sight,
And may not enter, having lost the key.
Yet surely I were more than man, or less,
Could I allure my hungry soul away
From such a spot, with such a power to bless,
And win not e'en what birds and fishes may :
At least I have the right of brutishness,
Who am in part an animal as they.

V

A WOODLAND STREAM, IV

FORGIVE me, gentle creatures of the stream,
And ye that in my fancy guard their bliss ;
Account me not a murderer, nor deem
My heart's offending darker than it is ;
The trespass in my thought is only this—
To ask a boon it doth not misbeseem
Your purity to grant, though well I wis
I am not worthy of a gift supreme.
Sinful I come from worlds where sin is rife,
But not with foul intent your peace to ban ;
I would but use the privilege of life,
And joy with Nature's joy while body can,
Yea, feel, in spite of all that breedeth strife,
Her spirit still has fellowship with man.

VI

IN THE MEADOW

THE Cuckoo called me, but I answered "Nay ;"
The Thrush said "Come," and I grew ill-content ;
Last spake the Blackbird ; then my heart forewent
Her studious purpose, and I broke the day.
Now in the meadow-grass, a world away
From aught of human life, that heart is blent
With leaf, stem, flower, in sweet entanglement,
Meshed by the young luxuriance of May,
The ox-eyed daisies glimpse me as I lie ;
Strange creeping things their devious steps have stayed,
And glut their wonderment from bloom and blade ;
While feathery balls are bending cubit-high
Between my quivering eyelids and the sky,
To mock me with a phantasy of shade.

G

VII

A RUSTIC BRIDGE, I

BLEST be the kindly heart of him who spanned
This sylvan streamlet with a bridge,—to me
Most grateful, and to all burnt souls who flee
For shelter from the torrid pasture-land.
Upon the slender plank I pause and stand,
Leaning hot arms upon the slender rail.
The foxglove-bloom I lately plucked looks frail
And like to wither in my feverish hand.
But here is sweet salvation,—rest and shade,
Awning of branches, every branch a bower,
And water for the sun-struck body's wound.
See! ferns and hemlock, and a shingle frayed
From pebbly banks, where the spread stream has power
To lave wood-flowers that droop with imminent swound.

VIII

A RUSTIC BRIDGE, II

INTO the stream I drop my foxglove-bell,
The rapid stream, the laughing leaping stream:
Through watery shades it throws a purple beam;
And each cool beast that drags a twisted shell
Beholds far off the palpitating swell,
And hears the runlet, brawling over stones,
Give murmurous thanks, like some old monk at Nones,
When the red sun makes drowsy-warm his cell.
So runs my fancy. But mine eyes have play
No deeper than the shining-shadowy floor;
The rest is secret as a moonless night.
Down floats my bell, away and still away,
Past the tall hemlock, round the fern-clad shore,
Beyond the reedy shallows, out of sight.

IX

POPPIES

O poppies in the meadow red and red,
And red and red through all the ripening corn,
I like the courage of that flaunting head
Which fronts the world so ragged, bold, and torn.
Why have our singers left your name unsaid,
Who might at least have flung you scorn for scorn,
Not passed you by to grieve unanswered,
And for pure lack of foemen grow forlorn?
See where I lift my hand to dash you dead—
What! is the joy of battle more than pain?
Nay, let us fight with angry words instead:
O cursèd flowers and vile, O stain and bane,
Go, turn your shameless faces to the bed!
Content ye yet,—or shall I strike again?

X

ON THE BEACH

When you lie there in such supreme content,
I feel a slight, a momentary pain,
Lest the strong heart so utterly unbent
Should take no more its ancient force again;
But, having fed on lotos-leaves, be fain
To feed so always, as on food god-sent,
And thus in Nature's paradise remain
A willing thrall to Nature's blandishment.
Dream on to-day, and fancy life a psalm
Best set to quiet melody of seas,
That meet on summer sands the summer breeze
To kiss the rising ripples into calm;
But when the morrow dawns, arise, appease
The natural craving of a strong right arm.

XI

FROM A QUIET PLACE

As when a maiden, looking through the leaves
That fence her garden from the common way,
Observes each passer-by, and softly weaves
A web of fiction, while her fancies play
Round each new figure; till she half believes
The tale so fashioned—tale which haply may
Be true, or if it pleasantly deceives,
No after-truth can dawn to counter-say:
So watch I from this world-sequestered nook
Time's heroes on the stage they tread so well,
Matching their motives with their outward look,
And run a single thread through all they do;
Nor would be told, what none is here to tell,
How much or little of my thought is true.

XII

SUBURBAN MEADOWS

How calmly drops the dew on tree and plant,
While round each pendulous leaf the cool airs blow!
The neighbour city has no sign to show
Of all its grim machines that toil and pant,
Except a sky that coal makes confidant:
But there the human rivers ebb and flow,
And thither was I wonted once to go
With heart not ill at ease or recusant.
Here now I love to wander morn and eve,
Till oaks and elms have grown oracular;
Yet conscious that my soberest thoughts receive
A tinge of tumult from the smoke afar;
And scarcely know to which I most belong—
These simple fields or that unsimple throng.

XIII

AN AUTUMN THOUGHT

It was a clear October morn.   The dell
After a frosty night lay thick with brown
Dead leaves.   And still they stirred and fluttered down,
Leaving a fringe against the sky to tell
Where once that sky had been invisible,
Cloaked by their green luxuriance.   And indeed
Mine eyes could notice how the vault, thus freed,
Grew bright and brighter for each leaf that fell.
So cuts the frost which kills our summer vows.
When shades of bliss we hoped eterne decay,
And all our pleasant leaves are stripped away,
We find what ampler view the frost allows.
Through earthly damps we catch the heavenly day,
And God's truth clearest under cold bare boughs.

XIV

TOWARDS EVENING

At morn we cried, "O pregnant hours of light,
What crystal thoughts declared in golden speech
Your lucid-lipped activities shall teach,
Ere sunset gives the glutted world to night !
All day we strove to learn, if learn we might ;
We groped for truth, but truth was hard to reach ;
A babble of tongues contended each with each,
'Mid blows that iron-fisted engines smite.
The day is gone.   Its voices garrulous
Have given us naught.   The void is yet to fill.
Shall not the silence prove more generous ?
The still eve comes : ah, let us too be still !
Our better thoughts are ever borne to us
On wings unfanned by any breeze of will.

XV

A CHANGE

You bid me sing !   Alas, the fount is dry
From which were drawn the songs you loved of old.
Long since I wandered from the field and fold,
And sought the tedious town, poor foolish I !
Even a true-born bard forgets the sky
When in the babbling street his days are told.
Free flows his verse to preach and teach and scold,
But fast his thoughts of beauty fade and die.
Sometimes a face may rouse him, or a child's
Soft prattle stir the genius at his heart.
Sometime his own brain's solitary wilds
Enclose him ; for a space he dwells apart.
But once enthralled to men and man's gross fashion,
He cnokes the spring-flood of his purest passion.

XVI

ON THE SUMMIT

Above the tarn, above the mantling wood,
My feet have gained at length the summit's pride,
Where cloud to peak, and peak to cloud, hath cried
Through countless years, " God is, and God is good."
O would that where I stand a thousand stood !
Such view to vision scarce pre-sanctified
Would more of God reveal than aught beside,
Yea, more than convent-cell or monkish hood.
For cloistered meditation needeth art
Beyond the narrow scope of common skill ;
But here the rudest, set the world apart,
Nearer to heaven by this fair height of hill,
Might trust the promptings of his natural heart
To worship, and consider, and be still.

XVII

ON THE BEACH IN NOVEMBER

My heart's Ideal, that somewhere out of sight
Art beautiful and gracious and alone,—
Haply where blue Saronic waves are blown
On shores that keep some touch of old delight,—
How welcome is thy memory, and how bright,
To one who watches over leagues of stone
These chilly northern waters creep and moan
From weary morning unto weary night.
O Shade-form, lovelier than the living crowd,
So kind to votaries, yet thyself unvowed,
So free to human fancies, fancy-free,
My vagrant thought goes out to thee, to thee,
As wandering lonelier than the Poet's cloud,
I listen to the wash of this dull sea

XVIII

SOMETHING LOST

How changed is Nature from the Time antique !
The world we see to-day is dumb and cold :
It has no word for us.   Not thus of old
It won heart-worship from the enamoured Greek.
Through all fair forms he heard the Beauty speak ;
To him glad tidings of the unknown were told
By babbling runlets, or sublimely rolled
In thunder from the cloud-enveloped peak.
He caught a message at the oak's great girth,
While prisoned Hamadryads weirdly sang :
He stood where Delphi's Voice had chasm-birth,
And o'er strange vapour watched the Sibyl hang ;
Or where, mid throbbings of the tremulous earth,
The caldrons of Dodona pulsed and rang.

THE CHILDREN'S PRIVILEGE

I LOVE to mark a childish band at play
Through flowerful meadows or a woodland scene :
The linnets in the copse are not so gay,
The squirrels in the forest not so keen :
They bear themselves with such ecstatic mien
As only masters of a Mystery may.
It moves my heart to think I too have been
In younger years initiate as they.
This Nature that we marvel at, and find
Impenetrable, is not so to them,
But opens half her secrets to their gaze,
And leads their footsteps in romantic ways ;
And none shall touch her garment's utmost hem,
Unless with childhood's unreflective mind.

XX

A VIEW

HERE is the hill-top. Look ! Not moor or fen,
Not wood or pasture, circles round the steep ;
But houses upon houses, thousand-deep,
The merchant's palace and the pauper's den.
We are alone,—beyond all mortal ken ;
Only the birds are with us and the sheep.
We are alone ; and yet one giant's-leap
Would land us in the flood of hurrying men.
If e'er I step from out that turbid stream
To spend an hour in thought, I pass it here :
For good it is across our idlest dream
To see the light of manhood shining clear ;
And solitude is sweetest, as I deem,
When half-a-million hearts are beating near.

XXI

SARK

O HAPPY Fate, which in the golden prime
Of this glad summer hast embarked my soul,
Despite her craven fears of rock and shoal,
And steered her safe to this delicious clime,
Where, careless of the World, and Life, and Time,
Beneath the sun-lit canopy of sky
She joys to watch the hours go floating by,
And find her fancies crisping into rhyme.
All day upon the cliff-top like a bird
I keep my nest, and lie in dreamful ease,
'Mid tall o'erarching grasses gently stirred
By the soft burden of the slumb'rous breeze—
The rhythmic plash of oarage faintly heard,
And long low murmur of the shoreward seas.

XXII

IN FEBRUARY

AT last! Through murk that seemed too thick for
    rending,
The sun has burst with full unclouded ray;
And hark, how soon the little birds are sending
Glad canticles from naked bush and spray.
Yet timidly; from time to time suspending
Their song, as if they feared to be so gay,
When every hour may bring the sunlight's ending
And all the gold relapse again to grey.
Pipe on, small songsters! You and I together
Will catch the passing glory while we may.
No Fate forbids to preen a drooping feather,
Give voice to hope, and try a broken lay.
What if the morrow break in wintry weather—
Is it not something that we sing to-day?

XXIII

IN THE CITY, I

A STRANGER, from the country's calm retreat
And heavenly boon of sweet tranquillity,
I tread with faltering steps the dusty street,
And seek in vain the God I long to see.
These traffickers who hold the world in fee—
They hurry past with such determined feet!
I seem to read in every face I meet,
"Am I not strong? What is thy God to me?"
He was so sweet to all the fields, so great
Among the hills, so fair in every glen,
So good to countless hungering eyes that wait
Upon His hand; I felt the Presence then—
Too distant now to cheer me desolate
In this grim weary wilderness of men.

XXIV

IN THE CITY, II

Nay, but thy God is near thee where thou wilt,
Not less nor more in solitude or crowd.
Take heart of grace, and go not heavy-browed,
Unless it be for consciousness of guilt.
God made the country; yea, but God hath built
All dwellings of his creatures, and endowed
Their lives with courage—else like water spilt
Upon the earth or as a melting cloud.
Haply they know it not, who never raise
A heavenward eye; they do the Giver wrong,
And yet He blesses. Thou with purer gaze
Shalt surely see the Arm that makes thee strong:
And if at times amid these murky ways
The vision pales, it will not be for long.

XXV

A COLLEGE FOR DECAYED MERCHANTS, I

He well deserved of Age and Broken Means,
Who planned in Mercy's cause this fair retreat.
His heart is dust; but still his pity leans
To succour those who faint with long-borne heat,—
Pale traffickers grown old in clamorous scenes,
Who sought the gold it was not theirs to meet;
Content at last to embrace such kindly screens
As shut the wearied from the vigorous feet.
The sober reds of tile and brick, the door
High-arched and crowned with shielded blazonries,
The little pillared court with stony floor,
Are eloquent of sweet tranquillities,—
And garden-ground expanding more and more,
With paths that wind amid perpetual trees.

XXVI

A COLLEGE FOR DECAYED MERCHANTS, II

Not seldom in these walks the Poet strolls,
And most when summer spreads her leaves; for then
Across the lawn his chair the cripple rolls,—
No bower but hath its agèd denizen:
And if from chapel-roof the slow bell tolls,
Saith Four-score-years to Three-score-years-and-ten,—
"We rest a college of immortal souls,
Albeit a company of dying men."
What time desire for calm has waxen deep,
And life's hot energies are all decayed,
I think it would be grateful here to sleep,—
I think it would be pleasant so to fade,—
With scarce a clock to tell how minutes creep,
And curtained by this venerable shade.

XXVII

A FOOTBALL PLAYER

If I could paint you, friend, as you stand there,
Guard of the goal, defensive, open-eyed,
Watching the tortured bladder slide and glide
Under the twinkling feet ; arms bare, head bare,
The breeze a-tremble through crow-tufts of hair ;
Red-brown in face, and ruddier having spied
A wily foeman breaking from the side ;
Aware of him,—of all else unaware :
If I could limn you, as you leap and fling
Your weight against his passage, like a wall ;
Clutch him, and collar him, and rudely cling
For one brief moment till he falls—you fall :
My sketch would have what Art can never give—
Sinew and breath and body ; it would live.

XXVIII

A CRICKET BOWLER

Two minutes' rest till the next man goes in !
The tired arms lie with every sinew slack
On the mown grass.   Unbent the supple back,
And elbows apt to make the leather spin
Up the slow bat and round the unwary shin,—
In knavish hands a most unkindly knack ;
But no guile shelters under this boy's black
Crisp hair, frank eyes, and honest English skin.
Two minutes only.   Conscious of a name,
The new man plants his weapon with profound
Long-practised skill that no mere trick may scare.
Not loth, the rested lad resumes the game :
The flung ball takes one madding tortuous bound,
And the mid-stump three somersaults in air.

XXIX

BEFORE THE RACE

The impatient starter waxeth saturnine.
" Is the bell cracked ? " he cries.   They make it sound :
And six tall lads break through the standers-round.
I watch with Mary while they form in line ;
White-jersey'd all, but each with some small sign,
A broidered badge or shield with painted ground,
And one with crimson kerchief sash-wise bound ;
I think we know that token, neighbour mine.
Willie, they call you best of nimble wights ;
Yet brutal Fate shall whelm in slippery ways
Two soles at least.   Will it be you she spites ?
Ah well !   'Tis not so much to win the bays.
Uncrowned or crowned, the struggle still delights ;
It is the effort, not the palm, we praise.

XXX

THE NEW CRICKET-GROUND

The loveliness of Earth is still unspent :
Her beauties, singly known, combined are strange :
And with what fondness she doth freshly range
Her ancient gems for man's new ravishment !
On this soft dew-fed tree-girt sward of Kent
The cricket-god to-day is first enthroned,
The dun herd banished, and its pasture owned
By white-clad players and their snowy tent.
The field I knew before, the lads I knew,
And oft elsewhere have watched their pleasant game ;
But now an added lustre comes to view,
Familiar features look no more the same ;
The new-set picture gains another hue,
And sheds another glory on its frame.

XXXI

A PALÆSTRAL STUDY

THE curves of beauty are not softly wrought :
These quivering limbs by strong hid muscles held
In attitudes of wonder, and compelled
Through shapes more sinuous than a sculptor's thought,
Tell of dull matter splendidly distraught,
Whisper of mutinies divinely quelled,—
Weak indolence of flesh, that long rebelled,
The spirit's domination bravely taught.
And all man's loveliest works are cut with pain.
Beneath the perfect art we know the strain,
Intense, defined, how deep soe'er it lies.
From each high master-piece our souls refrain,
Not tired of gazing, but with stretchèd eyes
Made hot by radiant flames of sacrifice.

XXXII

CHILDHOOD AND YOUTH

A CONTRAST

I LOVE to watch a rout of merry boys
Released from school for play, and nothing loth
To make amends for late incurious sloth
By wild activity and strident noise ;
But more to mark the lads of larger growth
Move fieldward with such perfect equipoise,
As if constricted by an inward oath
To scorn the younger age and clamorous joys ;
Prepared no less for pastime all their own,
A silent strenuous game of hand and knee,
Where no man speaks, but a round ball is thrown
And kicked and run upon with solemn glee,
And every struggle takes an earnest tone,
And rudest sport a sober dignity.

XXXIII

A REBUKE

DEAR friend, why takes your brow so dark a hue
Because these babes prefer a noisy bliss?
They laugh too loud perhaps; but surely 't is
A venial fault where merry sounds are few.
When you were young, the world was young with you;
Now you are old, and must you grieve for this—
That still the world is young, or take amiss
The sport of those to whom delight is due?
We press and strive and toil from morn till eve;
From eve to morn our waking thoughts are grim.
Were children silent, we should half believe
That joy was dead—its lamp would burn so dim.
But in one boy's halloo it finds reprieve,
And lives for us because it lives for him.

XXXIV

THE POWER OF CHILDHOOD

O CHILDREN, if the paradise our dream
Is found at all upon this earth we fret,
To you the glory and to us the debt
Must aye belong!   Forgive us if we seem
To hold our corded bales in more esteem.
The cares of market crowd our souls; and yet
In busiest hours we never quite forget
With what mild innocence your round eyes beam.
Give kisses, lest we grow too covetous
Of pilèd treasure on our dusty shelves:
Be near to guard when wealth is perilous,
For ye are strong and heaven-defended elves:
Lift up your lithe brown hands and pray for us,
Who dare not ask the cheapest boon ourselves.

XXXV

FLORA

SOME faces scarce are born of earth, they say;
Thine is not one of them, and yet 'tis fair;
Showing the buds of hope in soft array,
Which presently will burst and blossom there;
Now small as bells that Alpine meadows bear,—
Too low for any boisterous wind to sway.
Why should we think it shame for youth to wear
A beauty portioned from the natural day?
'T is thine to teach us what dull hearts forget,
How near of kin we are to springing flowers.
The sap from Nature's stem is in us yet;
Young life is conscious of uncancelled powers.
And happy they who, ere youth's sun has set,
Enjoy the golden unreturning hours.

XXXVI

BILL: A PORTRAIT

I KNOW a lad with sun-illumined eyes,
Whose constant heaven is fleckless of a cloud;
He treads the earth with heavy steps and proud,
As if the gods had given him for a prize
Its beauty and its strength.　What money buys
Is his; and his the reverence unavowed
Of toiling men for men who never bowed
Their backs to any burden anywise.
And if you talk of pain, of doubt, of ill,
He smiles and shakes his head, as who should say,
"The thing is black, or white, or what you will:
Let Folly rule, or Wisdom: any way
I am the dog for whom this merry day
Was made, and I enjoy it."　That is Bill.

XXXVII

FROM ANY POET

O FAIR and Young, we singers only lift
A mirror to your beauty dimly true,
And what you gave us, that we give to you.
And in returning minimise the gift.
We trifle like an artist brought to view
The nuggets gleaming in a golden drift,
Who, while the busy miners sift and sift,
Will take his idle brush and paint a few.
O Young and Glad, O Shapely, Fair, and Strong,
Yours is the soul of verse to make, not mar!
In you is loveliness : to you belong
Glory and grace : we sing but what you *are*.
Pleasant the song perchance ; but O how far
The beauty sung of doth excel the song !

XXXVIII

A STORY OF AURELIUS

WITH foliage gathered from the sacred bough
Young Marcus worshipped where the Salii dwell
Before the warrior-god he served so well,
What time they flung their garlands, striving how
They best might crown the statue's head.   And now
A strange thing happened (so the chroniques tell)—
The other chaplets missed their aim, and fell :
Only the boy's wreath lighted on the brow.
And was the god or passive or displeased ?
I think Parnassus joins Olympus here :
O hearts of youth, so brightly frankly true,
To gods and bards alike your praise is dear ;
Though wreaths from adult hands be all unseized,
Our crowns are crowns indeed if thrown by you !

H

XXXIX

A THOUGHT FROM PINDAR

NEM. V

Twin immortalities man's art doth give
To man; both fair; both noble; one supreme.
The sculptor beating out his portrait scheme
Can make the marble statue breathe and live;
Yet with a life cold, silent, locative;
It cannot break its stone-eternal dream,
Or step to join the busy human stream,
But dwells in some high fane a hieroglyph.
Not so the poet.   Hero, if thy name
Lives in his verse, it lives indeed.   For then
In every ship thou sailest passenger
To every town where aught of soul doth stir,
Through street and market borne, at camp and game,
And on the lips and in the hearts of men!

XL

VIRGIL

Not for the glittering splendour of thy verse,
O Seer-singer, do we count thee dear;
Not for the prowess of the Ænean spear,
The long brave battling with the Dardan curse;
But for thy human heart's sake we rehearse
Thy deep lines eloquent with hope and fear;
Thou too wert human; yea, to thee were near
The Fates that are about us and coerce.
Surely no softer subtler foot ere trod
Regions unlit save by the spirit's flame;
And through all shadows this high faith was thine:
Powerless is death to quench the spark divine;
Man's soul unfettered turneth whence it came;
God its fruition, for its seed was God.

XLI

IN THE CLOISTERS

WINCHESTER COLLEGE, I

I WALKED to-day where Past and Present meet,
In that grey cloister eloquent of years,
Which ever groweth old, yet ever hears
The same glad echo of unaging feet.
Only from brass and stone some quaint conceit,
The monument of long-forgotten tears,
Whispers of vanished lives, of spent careers,
And hearts that, beating once, have ceased to beat.
And as I walked, I heard the boys who played
Beyond the quiet precinct, and I said—
" How broad the gulf which delving Time has made
Between those happy living and these dead."
And, lo, I spied a grave new-garlanded,
And on the wall a boyish face that prayed.

XLII

IN THE CLOISTERS

WINCHESTER COLLEGE, II

Two things are ever with us, youth and death—
The Faun that pipes, and Pluto unbeguiled ;
From age to age still plays the eternal child,
Nor heeds the eternal doom that followeth.
Ah, precious days of unreflecting breath !
There lay (so might we fancy) one who smiled
Through all life's paradox unreconciled,
Enjoying years the grown man squandereth.
And if his latest hour was touched with pain,
And some dim trouble crossed his childish brain,
He knew no fear,—in death more blest than we.
And now from God's clear light he smiles again,
Not ill-content his mortal part to see
In such a spot, amid such company.

XLIII

TWO THOUGHTS

When I reflect how small a space I fill
In this great teeming world of labourers,
How little I can do with strongest will,
How marred that little by most hateful blurs,—
The fancy overwhelms me, and deters
My soul from putting forth so poor a skill:
Let me be counted with those worshippers
Who lie before God's altar, and are still.
But then I think (for healthier moments come),
This power of will, this natural force of hand,—
What do they mean, if working be not wise?
Forbear to weigh thy work, O soul!   Arise,
And join thee to that nobler sturdier band
Whose worship is not idle, fruitless, dumb.

XLIV

A BENEDICTION

Now may God bless thee for thy face, at least,
Seeing there is such comfort in the mere
Mute watching of it,—yea, a constant feast
Of golden glamour when the days are drear,
And summer harmonies have sunk and ceased.
This is the very death-day of the year;
Yet Beauty is not dead; thou art her priest,
Thy face her temple 'mid the shed leaves here.
And if for me no Spring should ever prank
My fields again with daisies anywhere,
And though all other faces dull and blank
Look through the darkness till they seem to bear
The guise of death, I cannot choose but thank
My God for having fashioned *one* so fair.

XLV

THE EXCUSE

If there were anything that I could do,
Which done would make your comfort more complete,
Think not I should continue this low seat,
And drink your bountihead as hitherto ;
Indeed I would most gladly toil for you :
And yet, believe me, it might happen, sweet,
That I should come in time to work my feat
For the feat's sake, forgetting whence it grew,
And so displacing love, should lose love so.
But since your life is full of things that bless,—
Dowered with such bounty that I may not guess
One smallest gift which man might still bestow,—
My Love hath leave to bloom in idleness,
And know herself with nothing else to know.

XLVI

A PLEA FOR DELAY

Not yet ! Not yet ! I dare not let thee go,
Till, line for line, thy face indelible
Lies printed on my heart as on a shell
That gravers cut for pearl-intaglio.
For one brief hour you will not grudge, I know,
To let my spirit, painter-fashion, dwell
Amid thy fronting lineaments, and tell
All that she learns in moving to and fro.
Remember, it may never chance again,
In this dim world of fates lethiferal,
That I alive should meet thee living too,
With power to mark thy traits as now I do ;
And lacking these, how would my soul retain
Thine image in the ways ethereal ?

XLVII

THE DYING PRINCE

HE was a monarch's son, and yet he lay
Racked by the latest pangs of long disease ;
And vainly through the lattice stole the breeze
To cool his fevered forehead, where Decay
Made broad her cruel image day by day ;
And vainly fell the shadow-gloom from trees,
At whose far feet the peasant droned at ease,
Rich in the sturdy health of common clay.
He saw the clouds.   He saw the smoke that curled
From lowly cots, the leaves that flecked his floor ;
The peacock screamed, cocks crew, the fountain purled,
And horses trampled at the castle-door ;
These were his tokens from the living world—
The world he might not visit any more.

XLVIII

A DREAM OF PICTURES

BY D. G. ROSSETTI

ONE soul through many windows looking out ;
One face transformed in vari-coloured moods,
But chiefly pale and sad, and framed about
With pansies plucked where Melancholy broods ;
A drooping spirit strengthened but to flout
Love's life-elixir ; faint, which yet eludes
All hands that succour ; and half-dead with drought
Remains enamoured of her solitudes.
Alas ! we may not help her.   She would turn
From our poor comfort, still disconsolate ;
Happy to be unhappy, glad to burn
With torturing flame which no tear-showers abate ;
Yea, rapt to heaven, unblest or blest too late,
In God's own presence still would yearn and yearn.

XLIX

AFTER TEN YEARS

A LEAGUE a-field with no intent of turning,
(One league or twain—God knows the world is wide,)
And fifty thoughts in fifty channels churning,
Ten years agone my fancy loved to ride;
The boy's young heart within me ever yearning
For stranger-truths to homely hearts denied;
There is so much that tempts us to the learning,
When Health's the horse and Youth is firm astride!
But Time is fleet for those who play the rover,
And lengthy jaunts corrupt to weary whiles;
'Tis strange to find, now riding days are over,
How great a space a little thought beguiles;
Enough at noon to amble through the clover,
And take the poppy-heads to mark the miles.

L

TO A WORKER RESIGNED

THE cry went forth for labourers in the field,
And thou, dear child, obedient to the cry,
Didst leave thy quiet home, with purpose high,
To lift strange implements thou couldst not wield.
Now, in the shadow of thy roof concealed,
Thou sittest lonely, thinking with a sigh,
Of blessèd deeds which stronger hands may try,
Of sad folk comforted, of sick folk healed.
Yet serve they not as well the common Lord
Who from one tiny circle never roam?
Doth not the glowworm on earth's humblest sward
Vie with the seraph in the starry dome?
Let others spread their soothing balms abroad;
Thou art the angel of the church at home.

LI

THE END OF IT

GIVE me your hand.   The glimmering star we sought
Has vanished wholly.   Truth is hard to find
In these fierce tournaments of mind and mind,
When thought leaps out to tilt with armèd thought,
And words are pierced and flung in angry sport.
We have forgotten why, forgotten how
We came to such rude cudgellings; and now
The brawl is everything, the end is naught.
Here sits no arbiter that Reason knows;
And Wisdom cries, "Surrender and be mute!"
I have no better friend than you,—suppose
Your love should cool, as logic grows acute!
Give me your hand.   We will no more dispute.
What boon hath strife that it should make us foes?

LII

IN A CHURCHYARD

WITH Thyrsis late I walked on holy ground,
And after silence at one tomb I spake:
"Here lies a man whose love no scorn could shake,
No toil could weary.   Though dull neighbours round
Observed him little as they mark this mound,
His goods, time, thought, were lavished for their sake,
His whole life spent in long attempt to make
The world he lived in nobler than he found.
And, Thyrsis, we at most can do no more:
That world outweighs us with the old blind stress.
Yet could we see him on the glittering shore,
The sheaves he carried might exceed our guess.
We keep the same great cause to labour for:
Look to it, Thyrsis, that we do no less."

LIII

TO ANY PAINTER

Be patient; take thy coloured threads, and weave
The robe of Beauty, flawless, without spot.
Be humble; what the world may grant, receive,
And yet for praise or guerdon lay no plot.
Be sober; though thy skill should win thee leave
To drain the bowl of Circé, use it not.
Be thankful; knowing there are those who grieve,
Because their genius has not gained thy lot.
The day thou servest may not be thy day:
It may not mark thee, bless thee, give thee gold
Or owning all thine art's imperial sway,
Refuse the lesson on thy canvas scrolled.
At least, when life is over, labour done,
One shall be nobler for the work of one.

LIV

TO AN INVALID

You ask me for a charm against disease —
Not of the body (you can bow to that),
But of the spirit, which you tremble at,
Lest it should dull your fine-wrought sympathies
With vigorous human life, and slowly freeze
The sinews of your mind, till they grow numb
As the dead limbs they live with, and become
Useless for all high purposes, like these.
What is my counsel? Choose a hero. Then
Make him your study,—temper, brain, and nerve,
Till he has grown your stronger self. And when
Weak morbid impulse comes on you to swerve
From the sane path, his grafted strength shall serve
To keep you true to God, your soul, and men.

LV

A PENITENT

Enough ! I choose to tell you.   Priest or no,
Your pity is grateful to me.   Yet be sure
For comfort's sake I tell you, not for cure.
Sin's pang is long in lessening,—not one throe,
Passed in a moment and forgotten so.
Nor do I dream (for that is Hell's own lure)
That we may fall, and afterwards grow pure
By much repenting.   Righteous we may grow,
Calm, steadfast, patient, peaceful if God bless,
Not pure,—not till the Last Day's trumpet-call,
When the round world shall learn our guiltiness,
And the maimed soul be stripped to all, that all,
Seeing the scar, may guess the fall, and guess
How great the Mercy which forgave the fall.

LVI

A PILGRIM

'Tis only perfect faith that never tires,
An angel trust that murmurs, " Come what may,
No fond regret shall tempt my feet to stray
From the strict path of mortified desires."
Though hearts are weak, lips need not so be liars.
Had there been any choice, I do not say
I should have chosen this dull rugged way,
This way of stones and flints, and wayside briars.
What then ?   I grieve not, faint not.   God is kind.
He gives me strange sweet flowers that push between
The flints,—such as no garden ever bore :
And gathering these, how can I choose but mind
What thankful hearts have gleaned where now I glean,
What patient feet have passed this way before ?

LVII

QUEM DI DILIGUNT

O KISS the almond-blossom on the rod !
A thing has gone from us that could not stay.
At least our sad eyes shall not see one day
All baseness treading where all beauty trod.
O kiss the almond-blossom on the rod !
For this our budding Hope is caught away
From growth that is not other than decay
To bloom eternal in the halls of God.
And though of subtler grace we saw no sign,
No glimmer from the yet unrisen star,—
Full-orbed he broke upon the choir divine,
Saint among saints beyond the golden bar,
Round whose pale brows new lights of glory shine—
The aureoles that were not and that are.

LVIII

BY A GRAVE-SIDE

HERE once again I stand, and once again
Recall thy beauty, O belovèd face,
And, O belovèd soul, thy gentle grace,
Thy flower of courtesy that knew not stain.
Thou art not here : yet is it sweetest pain
To think of thee in this the nearest place
Of earthly places to that spirit-space,
Which no man sees at all except he feign.
Forgive me that I may not often come
To mourn thee here, who mourn where'er I go,
Toiling to swell the Age's Beauty-sum,
Till in the lapse of Time's eternal flow,
Mine arm as thine is dead, my lips are dumb,
My head beside thy head is laid a-low.

LIX

ON READING A POET'S "LIFE"

BECAUSE he sang of pleasant paths and roses,
You thought that summer joys were all his care.
"The only wisdom," so you cried, "he knows is
How much delight one crowded day can bear :
The reason why his verse uniquely flows is
That he alone has wealth of bliss to spare :
In Tempé's vale for life he gathereth posies,
And flings the few he doth not keep to wear."
The veil is lifted now.   Behold your singer,—
A sick poor man, despised, and barely sane,
Who strove awhile to shape with palsied finger
The hard-wrung produce of a sleepless brain,
Rich but in throes,—till Death, the great balm-bringer,
Stooped down to kiss him through the deeps of pain.

LX

TO A MOTHER

WEEP not, O fond one, for thy wayward boy !
This foolish world is more to blame than he,
That takes the youngster on her nursing knee,
And makes him 'ware of whatso gawds destroy :
Then later, when he cries for some coarse toy,
Loosens her doting arms and lets him free,
And murmurs, "Fool !   And yet I will not see.
Did ever youth resist a glittering joy ? "
Take heart.   Though there be those who never learn,
Or learn too late, which is the better friend,—
Thy lad, of nobler mettle, shall not spurn
The love that saves while life is all to spend,
But wise betimes, awake, repent, return,
And bless thy patient pleading in the end.

LXI

TO A STRANGE TEACHER

TROUBLE me no more.   The world is very wide
And full of souls whose primal faith has fled.
Go first to them ; and leave one simple head,
Wherein the earlier teachings still abide.
Why seek to fill a mouth that has not cried,
To clog satiety of bread with bread ?
Can any hunger having richly fed ?
Can one be full, and yet dissatisfied ?
If I were wretched, you should perhaps prevail :
At least I might give ear to you.   But now,
Because I am so happy, and because
Content with life, I would be as I was,
Your message moves me not.   Who questions how
To dig new cisterns, till the elder fail ?

LXII

WINDOWS OF THE CHURCH

I. ST. MATTHEW

THIS form is Matthew ; sometime Publican,
But now God's Saint.   Who having sat long while
Receiving custom with no thought of guile,
Honest in stewardship, albeit by man
Despised, by God of place in His great plan
The nations and Himself to reconcile
Was held most worthy, yea of work and style
Desired by angels ere the world began.
For as on that bright day beside his board
He counted tribute, from the city-gate
Came One with strangest summons : "Follow Me."
'Twas Jesus, named of Nazareth.   And he,
Knowing his life new-called and consecrate,
Rose up,—the elect Historian of the Lord.

LXIII

II. ST. MARK

To Mark the second place ; that Mark who erst
Was kin to Barnabas and friend of Paul,
And reckoned it an easy thing and small
To be their yoke-fellow through lands accurst,
Preaching deliverance to the tribes dispersed ;
Yea, and was helpful ere his faith had fall ;
Then taking fearfulness for Heaven's recall,
Went back and walked not with them as at first ;
And so was lost to Paul, but not to God ;
Who bore him gently as a tender child,
Strengthened and blest him ; till with feet new-shod
Again he ventured on the pagan wild,
Carried the Light of lights from shade to shade,
Travailed, and suffered, and was not afraid.

III. ST. LUKE

HERE standeth Luke, Physician once, and still ;
Healer of souls whom God delights to save ;
Wise-eyed in helpfulness ; in pity brave ;
For all diseases using blessèd skill ;
To halt, maimed, blind, beneficent ; until
From town obscure by Galilean wave
Flashed forth the Day-Star, born of God, and gave
New life to suppliants with a sweet " I will."
At whose appearing Luke was straightly dumb,
Lost in the greater Light ; nor found it hard ;
But knelt and worshippèd ; and afterward
For thy monition, O Theophilus,
Wrote large his gospel, and for help of us,
On whom the last days of the world are come.

IV. ST. JOHN

BEHOLD the face that Jesus loved of yore, *1*
The face of John.   Long time with Zebedee
He dragged his rough nets through the darkling sea :
Till Jesus marked the power unmarked before,
And called him from his black boat on the shore
To fish for men.   With zeal and lovingly
He did that fisher-work, while hands were free ;
Then lived God's prisoner, and was blest yet more ;
Who on a day in Patmos knew the whirl
Of spirit-wings around him, (it is writ
To them that held him as Evangelist,)
And saw God's City, and the walls of it—
All gems, from jasper up to amethyst,
With streets gold-glass, and every gate a pearl.

LXVI

THE TORCH-BEARER

1

IN splendour robed for some court-revelry
A monarch moves when eve is on the wane.
His faithful lieges flock their prince to see,
And strive to pierce the gathering shade—in vain.
But lo, a torch !   And now the brilliant train
Is manifest.   Who may the bearer be ?
Not great himself, he maketh greatness plain.
To him this praise at least.   What more to me ?
Mine is a lowly Muse.   She cannot sing
A pageant or a passion ; cannot cry
With clamorous voice against an evil thing,
And break its power ; but seeks with single eye
To follow in the steps of Love her King,
And hold a light for men to see Him by.

LXVII

THE POET

WHAT is a Poet?   Is he one who keeps
His heart remote from cares of human-kind,
Tasting the rich feast of a perfect mind,
Watching the shadowed Form that broods and sleeps
On Fancy's breast, and drawing from her deeps
New thoughts of Beauty, splendid, unconfined ;
Contemptuous of the common lot, and blind
To the great silent crowd that toils and weeps?
Ah, no!   All woes that all men ever knew
Lie in his soul, their labours in his hand ;
Yea, tear for tear, and haply tear for smile,
Sin's smile, he renders them ; and if some while
He doth withdraw himself, 'tis but to stand
Such space apart as gives the larger view.

LXVIII

THE ART THAT ENDURES

MARBLE of Paros, bronze that will not rust,
Onyx or agate,—Sculptor, choose thy block !
Not clay nor wax nor perishable stock
Of earthy stones can yield a virile bust
Keen-edged against the centuries.   Strive thou must
In molten brass or adamantine rock
To carve the strenuous shape which shall not mock
Thy faith by crumbling dust upon thy dust.
Poet, the warning comes not less to thee !
Match well thy metres with a strong design.
Let noble themes find nervous utterance.   Flee
The frail conceit, the weak mellifluous line.
High thoughts, hard forms, toil, rigour,—these be thine,
And steadfast hopes of immortality.

LXIX

WORDS AND THOUGHTS

O words are weak! We need a stronger tongue
To utter forth the heart's imaginings.
Our deepest deep is full of subtle things,
Things mystic, marvellous,—unsaid, unsung,
Because they may not anywise be wrung
Into a verbal mode. So no man brings
To upper light his soul's hid travailings,
Or tells what stars his spirit moves among.
And yet, God knoweth, it might well be worse,
(Since life is gone if all its fruits are gone,)
Could we not keep, when formal thoughts disperse,
Some half-revealèd shape to search and con,
Some child of Fancy's children still at nurse,
Some brede of Love for Love to brood upon.

LXX

AN APOLOGY

I hold not lightly by this world of sense,
So full it is of things that make me cheer.
I deem that mortal blind of soul and dense,
To whom created joys are less than dear.
The heaven we hope for is not brought more near
By spurning drops of love that filter thence:
In Nature's prism some purple beams appear,
Of unrevealèd light the effluence.
Then count me not, O yearning hearts, to blame
Because at Beauty's call mine eyes respond,
Nor soon convict me of ignoble aim,
Who in the schools of Life am frankly fond;
For out of earth's delightful things we frame
Our only visions of the world beyond.

I

THIRTY SONNETS

NOT INCLUDED IN THE 1885 VOLUME

LXXI

LIFE

WHITE sails that on the horizon flash and flee,
A moment glinting where the sun has shone ;
White billows for a moment riding free,
Then gulfed in other waves that follow on ;
White birds that hurry past so rapidly,
Albeit no sight more bright to look upon ;
Like you our little life ; we are as ye—
A moment sighted, in a moment gone.
Yet not in vain, oh, not in vain, we live,
If we too catch the sunlight in the air,
And signal back the beauty ere we sink
In that dark hollow men call death, and give
To saddened souls that watch us on the brink
A gleam of glory, transient but fair.

LXXII

TO A STUDENT

IT is enough, O straining Heart and strong,
Enough that in thy safely-garnered store
Thou hast heaped high the rich and varied lore
Of dead decades.   Thou dost thy scholars wrong
To keep them waiting for the light so long.
And nature swoons.   Oh, what if nevermore
The face of man looks human as of yore,
And mute for thee grows melody of song ?
These things are more than learning ; these are life.
The Past is grand ; but is he wise who deems
All else ignoble ? Spite of sound and strife,
To-day is not so barren as it seems.
Thou mightest know an angel in thy wife,
And fair child-faces looking through thy dreams.

LXXIII

AT THE ISTHMIAN GAMES

We crown thee, Hero, not for strength alone ;
That were a meed unworthy thy desert.
Strength in the base is objectless, inert,
Or strained to keep some passion on its throne.
We crown thee rather, for that thou hast shown
How fair thy prowess, and how fitly girt
With laurel is the strength which does no hurt
To the heart's image of ideal tone.
Rough men our eyes have wondered at ere now,
Who ran with wingèd feet as thou hast run ;
Others we know—tall youths with graceful brow
Inviting wreaths of bay, yet wearing none
Because their feet move sluggishly.   But thou
Hast given us strength and beauty joined in one.

LXXIV

IN THE SOPHIST'S AKADEMÊ :
AN IDLER

The old man babbles on.   Ye gods, I swear
My soul is sick of these philosophers !
In sooth I marvel that young blood should care
To hear such vapid stuff : yet no one stirs.
Who's for a breath of unpolluted air ?
See yonder brown-eyed nursling of the Muse,—
I'll pluck his robe and ask him ; if he choose,
We two can steal away and none be ware.
What joy to find a woodland rill, and wade
Knee-deep through pebbly shallows ; then to lie
With glistening limbs along the open glade,
And let the soft-lipped sunbeams kiss them dry :
Or wandering in the grove's remoter shade
To sport and jest and talk—philosophy !

LXXV

THE SAME CONTINUED

He will not come. Poor fool! no thought of fun
Lights his dark soul—content in this drear place
To spend the golden hours in fruitless chase
Of witless words. How softly one by one
The breezes fold their wings till day be done;
The laurels droop; from out the pillar's base
A grass-green lizard peeps with wrinkly face,
And turns his beaded eyes toward the sun.
Look east. I think god Phœbus never shone
More brightly on the Mount. A molten bar
Leaps from Athenê's helm as from a star,
Wakes the white spirit of the Parthenon,
Then dies upon the purple hills afar
In flame. And still the old man babbles on.

LXXVI

A PHILISTINE

Yestre'en while strolling through a marish dale
I marked a thistle-feeding ass, and said:
" Poor patient drudge, how will thy worth avail
To lift thy name, while thou art thistle-fed?
See, here are cytisus and galingale—
Blooms of Theocritus; crop these instead:
So haply may some Genius in thy head
Throb gloriously and tingle through thy tail.
Then would men credit thee with breadth of brain
Beyond thy race, and thou 'mong all that dwell
In British donkeydom shouldst bear the bell."
He paused; I showed the sacred food; in vain!
His lumpish nose turned thistlewards again.
"Thou wast fore-doomed," I murmured; " fare thee
    well!"

LXXVII

A PHILOSOPHER

THE fire burns bright; the kettle in the grate
Sends gentle music floating through the air,
While Rumpelstilzchen* from the easy chair
Makes soft refrain.　O friend, serene, sedate,
Thou hast a strange capacity to bear
The good and evil of a changing state;
Thrice-happy thus voluptuously to fare,
Yet not remorseful if unkindly Fate
Appoints cold vigils in a leafless tree.
Brave Stoic-epicure!　Would I might win
Some part of thy combined philosophy;
Enjoy beatitude without a sin,
Yet take my crosses kindly; live like thee,
All fur without, and triple brass within.

LXXVIII

DEDICATION TO "THE WINDOWS OF THE CHURCH"

TO MISS F. C. L.

THIS is a tiny Book: yet here is writ
An honoured name, as those who know it know.
Hath blind conceit inscribed it then?　Not so.
Yon vane that on the steeple-top doth sit,—
How small it is, how slender, weak, unfit
For noble ends!　But while its hand can show
With faithful point which way the breezes blow,
Men are content, and ask no more of it.
And this my little Book is such a vane;
Void in itself of strength or dignity;
But set where all who choose may see it plain;
And mark, O gentle Head, how constantly,
In summer sunshine or through winter rain,
The love-winds of my reverence tend to Thee.

* One of Southey's favourite cats was so called.

LXXIX

A DISCIPLE SECRETLY, I

One glance upon the dead face,—only one.
You think it strange ; but he can never know ;
Or with a spirit's knowledge would he shun
Last look from any friend who loved him so
As I have loved : in happy mood and low,
In hours of grave content, in hours of fun,
In mind's debate, in full heart's overflow,
Through all his course, till all his course was done.
What if I spake but little,—did not tell
The wealth of reverence ever waxing more
As he grew worthier worship ?   Is it well
To pluck a secret from the heart's hid core,—
Play thief where Self-respect as sentinel
Keeps watch upon a still unopened door ?

LXXX

A DISCIPLE SECRETLY, II

Nay, surely ; Love must know her times, and whom
She will, confesses.   Can the budding flower,
When hasty fingers break it unto bloom,
Match the bright offspring of a natural hour,
That warmed by sun, and woke by sudden shower,
Expands full-orbed ?   Albeit, if subtle doom
Eclipse its beauty unfulfilled, no power
Shall curl its petals skyward from the tomb.
I did not speak.   Is that a reasoned grief,
Now chance of speech is gone, for ever gone ?
What could I give ?   A flower in broken leaf,
A thing his eye would scarcely gaze upon,
And Head had cried to Heart, "O foolish Thief
To steal what should be fairly thine anon !"

LXXXI

DREAM-TRAVEL

At night on Fancy's moon-lit main
I launch my shallop, like a thief
From doom of Justice fugitive,
If haply I may glide and gain
The land whereof sad hearts are fain,
Where lotos hangs a heavy leaf,
And amaranth is grown for grief,
For grief that is no longer pain ;
And human tongues are like a tune
Heard faintly through the dusk of June,
As though in some unearthly grot,
Where Fate and Force and Fear are not,
A silver-throated choir did sing
To softest note of pshawm-playing.

LXXXII

ISABEL: A PORTRAIT

Who loves a deep face, let him look with me
On this of Isabel's,—to common sight
Perfect in paleness, wonderful and white,
But to the studious gaze a mystery :
For never calm so utter save there be
A home of turbid feelings recondite,
Though none shall find it in the soul's despite,—
Few guess it under such tranquillity.
She is a passion-flower hung overhead,
That will not stoop its disc for eyes to see ;
A scriptured lily, ere its petals spread,
Shut close until the sunshine,—so is she ;
Fair riddle not by all men to be read ;
Bright casket opening to one special key.

LXXXIII

THE HONEY-MOON

Till dusk crept o'er the June-grass round my seat,
She lay and listened, drinking word by word
All the old tales of Arcady that spurred
The Doric heart, and made Greek pulses beat.
I could have talked for aye : it was so sweet
To mark her up-turned face, while night's one bird
Woke in the beech, and eve's last zephyr stirred
And sighed a little, ere it sank effete.
At length she rose with forehead sagely knit :
" It never was," she cried—"that age divine ! "
And I : " But how then could we dream of it ?
As well deny yon far-off tapers shine."
And so we passed to household lamps new-lit,
My hand upon her shoulder, hers on mine.

LXXXIV

A POETASTER

Of common things I treat in scanty rhymes,
My verse is wrung from life's familiar prose,
I hardly guess if Hippocrene still flows,
'Tis not my wit that Helicon sublimes.
Like that rude peasant-lad of mythic times,
I press my beanstalk with illiterate toes,
Not envious of the learnèd wight who knows
A lordlier stair perchance,—and never climbs.
Or change the trope ; my lines are coined of stuff
That lay where no Scamander richly rolled.
From native soil, obscure, unvalued, rough,
I dig the metal for my sonnet-mould.
It melts, it runs, it sparkles—'tis enough !
Men call it copper : well, I dream it gold.

LXXXV

AN EVENING WALK

At fall of night we wandered forth to muse,
And arm in arm pursued the shadowy lane,
Careless where Fate might lead, or Fancy choose
To draw our footsteps in her silver chain.
Enough to know the grandeur overhead,
And feel the voiceless music of the hour,
That symphony which wakes responsive power
In every heart of man not wholly dead :
Or even dead, what heart but lives again,
Recalled to being by so sweet a strain ?
At times like this, the outer air is fraught
With some soft spell, which moves to harmony
The human soul within, till all our thought
Is touched with pathos—and we know not why

LXXXVI

SHELLEY

Some men are nature wise—yet cannot pray ;
Scan leaf and stone, and know not that they drink
God's air at every breathing ; souls that sink
Whelmed in the billow while they mark the spray,
Blind to the death.   This man did more than they ;
Got faith, and travelled to the very brink
Of the great world's great secret, as I think ;
Then losing faith, fell back, and missed his way.
Happier the child who knows that God is good :
He only knew that God's great work is fair.
Yet he loved much, and in sublimer mood
Might live and worship in that tranquil air
Where all is seen, all told, all understood ;
Haply our mazèd souls shall meet him there.

LXXXVII

THE LIGHT OF THE WORLD

" BEHOLD I stand!"   Who standeth?   Can it be
The Son of God, the Christ, the crucified,
Whom thou hast all thy life contemned, denied,
And thrust asunder?   Yea, 'tis even He.
"Behold, I stand and knock!"   Where knocking?   See
The closèd door thick-set with thorns of pride,
And choked with idle weeds from side to side ;
It is the door of thine impiety.
"Behold, I stand and knock.   If any hear
My voice and open" (Foolish soul, to thee
He speaketh all night long.   Dost thou not fear
To keep Him waiting there so wearily ?),
"I will come in," (O God, my God, how near !)
"Yea, and will sup with him, and he with Me."

LXXXVIII

AUTUMN LEAVES

How soft they fall !   No fevered clutch.
No frenzied prayer, no fruitless vow !
They wait the doom with fearless brow :
Death is not terrible to such.
Thus let me die—not striving much
To keep my hand upon the bough,
When Fate comes near with friendly touch,
And whispers, " Life is over now " ;
Still less receive, as loth to go,
The summons with a fret or frown ;
But learn from this calm end to know
How patient faith may fitly crown
A life uncrownèd else ; and so,
In shade or sun, drop gently down.

LXXXIX

A LATE SPRING

THE wintry blast that chills, the frost that nips,
Match well this most un-spring-like vault of grey,
The sun has suffered long a cloud eclipse,
And all the merriment gone out of May.
Where are the blue-bells, where the cowslips, where
The song of nightingales, the cuckoo's note?
No voice is heard from any feathered throat,
No beds of early blossom scent the air.
So spake I yesterday : and, lo, this morn
Unveiled a sun now blazing on to noon!
The looked-for babe of vernal hope is born,
And means to leap from out his cradle soon.
O patient Earth, put on thy robe and sing!
The skies are clear; at length, at length 'tis Spring.

XC

TO E. C. P.

You do me wrong, my friend.   I never said
That fault of heart is screened by charm of face,
Or bade you look for love, then take instead
A thin veneer of superficial grace.
I did but amplify a common thought,
That light without is born of flame within,
That pure and noble lines of feature ought
To image forth a soul unmarred by sin.
There is a formal beauty all of earth,
A poor deceptive thing of little worth;
Of that I spake not.   To the Poet's eye
One God illumes all good since Time began;
The rest he looks on but in passing by
To realise the perfect type of man.

XCI

ADVICE

If I were you, with health and youth in touch—
Great gifts at hand, and greater gifts in store,
I would not, for the much, forget the more,
I would not, for the more, neglect the much.
Be rich to-day ; but while to-day you clutch
The fruit which yesterday your hands forbore,
Bethink you of the days that stretch before,
And spare the seed which shall be fruit for such.
Not all to spend, nor all to save, is best ;
To have, to hope ; to enjoy, and still pursue ;
To climb awhile, and then awhile to rest ;
To love the old, and yet acclaim the new ;
And " Good the goal " should be my creed confest,
If I were you, dear lad,—if I were you !

XCII

SIBYL'S HAND

There are five fingers in a hand, I think ;
And Sibyl's hand hath neither less nor more :
To wit, a thumb, a common thumb, and four
Well ordered digits fleshed in white and pink,
As other digits are.   Yet when I link
My hand in hers, as daily in a score
Of hands I link it, steals through every pore
A strange sweet feeling not with pen and ink
Definable,—so strange indeed and sweet
That I can scarce quit hold.   Now tell me pray,
Good friends discreet of soul,—when next we meet
And Sibyl smiles, which is the better way—
Shall I refuse the hand stretched out to greet,
Or clasp and keep it ever and a day ?

XCIII

SAINTS

O SAINTS, dear Saints, so present, yet so far!
I cannot touch you with my hand, or trace
The aspect of your strength, your faith, your grace;
Between us lie the years,—the gulf, the bar.
But as one tracks the starlight to the star,
And finds no dark nor flame-forsaken space
To fret the beauty of its burning face,
Because the splendour swallows blot and scar;
So Time has framed you with an aureole
More circle-rounded than your age foreknew;
No frailty now can quench that fire of soul!
The things ye willed, and did not, those ye do;
The gifts ye strove for, in my sight are true;
Your perfect parts have made perfection whole.

XCIV

ON A DULL DOG

THIS dog was dull.   He had so little wit
That other dogs would flout him, nose in air.
But was he therefore wretched?   Did he care
How dogdom snarled, or even think of it?
He thought of nothing, but all day would sit
Warm in the sun, with placid vacant stare,
Content, at ease, oblivious, unaware;
And all because—he had so little wit!
O happy dulness which is dull indeed,
And cannot hear the critic-world's "Go hang!"
Small bliss we get from our too-conscious breed,
We semi-dullards of the middle gang!
To mark the rose, and know one's-self a weed,
And know that others know,—there lies the pang!

XCV

THE CARPET-WEAVER

LIVED once a carpet-weaver, poor in purse
But rich in love for all things fair, and all
That lift the soul.   Hard fortune !   Did he curse
The sordid Fates that bound him to the stall ?
He reared his booth against the temple wall,
Marked every day the wreathèd crowds disperse,
Heard flute and tabor and the doves' low call
And wove meanwhile his carpets—think you, worse ?
We may not all be temple-slaves of Art ;
The world has ruder work for you, for me.
Yet so God lets us toil, that, pure in heart,
We dimly guess what happier eyes can see ;
What happier lips can sing is ours in part,
If we keep time with their sweet minstrelsy.

XCVI

FAITH AND LOVE

THE darkened chamber held the maiden dead.
Her name was Faith.   Of long neglect she died.
And now men rose and shook themselves and cried,
" O Faith, come back,—come back ere Hope be fled ! "
But she lay silent on her solemn bed,
And men grew piteous at their prayer denied ;
They said " No more is man to man allied ;
We fall asunder—and the world," they said.
And while they talked, behold a gracious form,
And Love beside the pillow bending low :
" We live and die together, she and I."
So then he kissed her, and her flesh grew warm ;
She woke and faced them with a ruddy glow.
If Love be living, Faith can never die.

April 1891.

K

XCVII

REVERENCE

BEHOLD, and touch not ; worship, and refrain.
Kneel in the outer court, nor hotly bring
Too near the Radiance thy frail offering,
Which is thyself.   Fond heart, what couldst thou gain
By creeping closer ?   Nay ; let be ; remain ;
Between thy love and the Belovèd thing
Keep still a space for rapt imagining,
Lest languor seize thee, and a subtle pain.
Thou art a man.   Be human and content.
Not thine to breathe a supersensual air
Or snatch the heart of bliss.   Thy joys are lent
To teach thee how to greet them and to spare :
As some grey prophet with his head low bent
Will give to Beauty blessing—all he dare.

   April 1891.

XCVIII

THE BEST ANSWER

SAY on.   You know how dead-alive I am.
Some men would wince to see their idols flung
From dim-lit darkness where so late they hung,
And turned adrift for jeers, and labelled "sham."
But I (you know me), mild as any lamb,
Give up my heroes to your slashing tongue,
Give up my martyrs to be burned and hung,
And keep my lips, and bless not, if you damn.
And when at length the wordy storm has waned,
Still bright the sky !   The rifted clouds reveal
The same unchanging sun.   Two things are gained.
My heart is tempered to a firmer steel,
And your true self comes out to soothe and heal.
But since you stirred me not, I am not pained.

   April 1891.

XCIX

RATAPLAN

"O Rataplan ! It is a merry note,
And, mother, I'm for 'listing in the morn ;"
"And would ye, son, to wear a scarlet coat,
Go leave your mother's latter age forlorn ?"
"O mother, I am sick of sheep and goat,
Fat cattle, and the reaping of the corn ;
I long to see the British colours float ;
For glory, glory, glory, was I born !"
She saw him march. It was a gallant sight.
She blest herself, and praised him for a man.
And straight he hurried to the bitter fight,
And found a bullet in the drear Soudan.
They dug a shallow grave—'twas all they might;
And that's the end of glory. Rataplan !

    April 1891.

C

THE INQUISITOR

Yes, pain is grievous ; *argumentum stat.*
But not so frightful as the flames of—well,
You know. And by compare, as schoolmen tell,
These pangs are scarce the stinging of a gnat.
Besides, we have the Church's mandate—flat !
"Compel them to come in,"—I say—"compel !"
Now if through naughtiness the flesh rebel,
And need sharp goading, dare we shrink from *that ?*
No, no ; last week a heretic we tried
Who much annoyed us, being obstinate
Beyond the measure of his kind. We plied
All engines ; [   ] for his sin was great.
Then I took unction just before he died
And sent him pardoned through St. Peter's gate.

    April 1891.

(This Sonnet, which is unfinished, was the last written by Lefroy.)

LYRICAL POEMS

AT LYNMOUTH

Sunny sky o'er sunny sea,
  Tiny waves that ripple in,
Where beside the little quay
  Rattles down the noisy Lyn ;
Rugged rocks that overhead
  Blend and blazon every hue,
Glowing purple, blushing red
  At the sea's diviner blue ;
Did your pencil ever paint,
Any picture half as quaint,
    Half as lovely, half as sweet,
      Marguerite ?

Deep sequestered, tree-begirt,
  In the vale the village sleeps,
Fenced around and screened from hurt
  By the crag-surmounted steeps ;
Under eaves white roses smile,
  Gable-high the fuchsia climbs,
Ruddy-tinted roofs of tile
  Peep from out the leafy limes ;
Of all Edens 'neath the sun,
Found or fancied, is there one
    More enchanting, more complete,
      Marguerite ?

Let us wander hand in hand
  Out of shadow into light,
View the beauties of the land
  From this bare unwooded height ;
Hill and valley, rock and rill,
  All in rich profusion lie,
Rock and river, vale and hill
  Stretched before the dazzled eye ;

Could the storied Isles of Bliss
Shew a scene as fair as this
    Here unfolded at our feet,
      Marguerite ?

Now descending let us pass
    Far from sight and sound of men,
Where the fern and scented grass
    Carpet soft the shaded glen ;
Where the river in its flow,
    Leaping down with merry glee,
Finds a sister stream, and, lo !
    Greets and bears her to the sea.
Lovely spot ! who would not stay,
Learning all the live-long day
    Lessons from this " waters-meet,"
      Marguerite ?

July 1876.

AUTUMN LEAVES

O LEAFLETS, old and brown and sere,
 It is full time to quit your bough ;
The autumn visage of the year
 Is frowning on you even now.
  Farewell !
How sad the tale ye tell
 Of summer past we know not how,—
Bright minutes fled beyond recall,
 And scarcely used, if used at all !

The northern breeze will thin your crown,
 And cut the laggards with his knife ;
Contending blasts will hurl you down,
 The victims of their windy strife.
  Frail things !
And yet from death forth-springs
 The promise of another life ;
Your very selves in altered guise
 Again shall smile to sunny skies.

October 1876.

TO A MAIDEN WHO WISHES TO
DRESS A LA MODE

O LET me love thee as thou art,
    Not as thou mayest be,
If twenty toilet-tricks impart
    A fancied grace to thee.
So many simple charms are blent
    Beneath that witching eye,
The soul that is not thus content
    Is hard to satisfy.

And wherefore try such doubtful ways?
    What dost thou seek to gain?
To bind a lover in whose gaze
    Each other maid is plain?
If all the nymphs of Gaul combine
    To deck thee with their store,
My heart's already wholly thine,
    I cannot give thee more.

Then ever leave such borrowed plumes
    To birds that doubt their own,
Assured that she is blest who blooms
    With nature's grace alone.
Thou least of all hast need to boast
    A loveliness suborned;
The beauty which entrances most
    Is beauty unadorned.

October 1876.

ODE

*On a prospect (*not *distant) of being ploughed a second time*

O PLOUGH, it is long since I met you,
   So cruelly keen in the " schools,"
But still I could never forget you,
   " Forget " is the tonic of fools.

Ah, then I was youthful and tender,
   And yours was a terrible name ;
If my knowledge of grammar was slender,
   I still kept a feeling of shame.

Afresh you would like to make tingle
   Every nerve in my system : in vain !
Your triumph is over,—'twas single ;
   You cannot enjoy it again.

To-day I am tougher and older,
   My freshness has vanished, and now,
With a back that is hard as a boulder,
   I laugh at your malice, O Plough !

November 1876.

TO AMARYLLIS

I LOVE thee with a love so deep
    And in its depth so strong,
Its spells transmute life's thorns to fruit,
    And sorrows into song.
For Beauty dead I could not weep,
    She cannot die to me ;
I love thee with a love so deep,
    So strong my love for thee.

I love thee with a love so rich,
    That in its charm so rare,
E'en Midas' self had left his pelf,
    And for thy sake gone bare ;
And yet not bare with half a niche
    In Eros' fane near thee ;
I love thee with a love so rich,
    So rare my love for thee.

I love thee with a love so true,
    And in its truth so tried,
That ere it pale life's force must fail,
    Or Time roll back his tide.
By slow degrees the sapling grew,
    Not quickly bends the tree ;
I love thee with a love so true,
    So tried my love for thee.

I love thee with a love that is
    The best of loves that are,—
A lustrous stone, which shines alone
    'Mid lesser lights a star ;
A star that adds to very bliss
    Another glint of glee ;—
I love thee with a love like this,—
    O what's thy love for me ?

January 1877.

RONDEAUS

IN THE MANNER OF MR. AUSTIN DOBSON

I

When Phillis frowns, an ugly blight
Descends where all before was light,
    Steals o'er the sunshine of her face,
    And quite eclipses half the grace
Wherewith the queenly maid is dight.

Her faëry guards in very fright
Unfold their wings, and take to flight;
    Creatures of earth and air give place,
    When Phillis frowns.

I may not—would not, if I might,—
Behold at large the woeful sight.
    Let Nature's healing sleep efface
    Unlovely lines in soft embrace:
Sweet Day, adieu! Come, gentle Night,
    When Phillis frowns!

II

O Love, how fair thou art to-day—
I would thy face were so alway!
    O Love, how fair thou art; and yet
    How apt, O Love, to play coquette,
As if the part were sweet to play.

At times as bright and blithe and gay
As ripples in the coral bay,—
    Without foreboding or regret,—
    O Love, how fair!

At times; but 'tis not always May,
And when thy votaress, Miss A.
     Makes up with *him* for whist a set,
     Or trills with *him* the soft duet,
'Tis not so easy *then* to say,
     " O Love, how fair ! "

III

To see His face is all her prayer ;—
To see His face,—no matter where :
     The sight of e'en the faintest trace
     Would glorify a desert-place,
And make the wilderness look fair.

The heaviest burden Love could share,
The direst peril Love would dare,
     If only for a little space
        To see His face.

Not yet, not here; Sweet soul, forbear
To fret for one beyond thy care.
     With hope assured, take heart of grace :
     The wheels of Time roll on apace ;
When death comes nigh, look up, prepare
        To see His face.

IV

FORGET-ME-NOT ! How Nature rears
Emblems of human hopes and fears
     Under our feet ! See where they grow,
     The tiny flowers that lovers know.
And fame of old romance endears.

We part to-night ! the moment nears ;
Here is a blossom dewed with tears.
    Reject it,—well !   Accept, and so
        Forget me not !

Either let fate produce the shears,
And nip the bond that disappears ;
    Forget me now before you go,—
    Or take the gift my hands bestow,
And then, through all the length of years
        Forget me not !

May 1878.

THE DEAD POET

Blow the trumpet loud and clear;
Blow, and yet 'tis somewhat late.
Could the sound have reached his ear,
His had been a happier fate.

While we had him, what his guerdon?
Wormwood rendered for his song,
Till he sank beneath the burden,—
You have waited over-long.

Gold and glory heaped for many,
Not a kindly word for him;
Ah! he would have blessed a penny,
When the light of life was dim.

Words that might have cheered, unspoken,
Shouted now, but all in vain;
If the silver cord be broken,
Is it ever joined again?

Call him noble, call him brave,
Call him genius, if you will;
But to call him from his grave
Far transcendeth all your skill.

May 1878.

VALEDICTORY

TO H. M. H.

FAREWELL! you pass to western lands
   Across the weary waste of sea,
In heart aglow with eager hands
   To seize the life which is to be.

Amid the work you go to find
   Upon that other busy shore,
You may not often bring to mind
   The finished course that went before.

But we at home shall oft recall
   A love in deed so firm and true,
And if you think of us at all,
   So think as we shall think of you.

At last return when life is low,
   And find a corner vacant yet
In hearts that loved long years ago,
   And never will, or can, forget.

L

IS IT SO?

Is it so?   Yester-eve, did you say,
He was taken away,
Without semblance of mercy or ruth
In the bloom of his youth,
Away from the hopes and the fears
Of young passionate years,
And the promise of strength as he grew
To his prime—is it true?

Very hard it must seem to the man
With a cut-and-dried plan
Of creation, which quite supersedes
All the time-honoured creeds,
And allots to each being a sphere
Which is pleasantly clear
While he holds his own place in the rank;—
If he dies, there's a blank.

But to you who are not narrow-brained
Does it seem unexplained,
Unsolved, like a riddle, this end,
This death of our friend?

Oxford.

HEROISM: A THOUGHT

Thou wouldst be Hero? Wait not then supinely
For fields of fine romance which no day brings
The finest life lies oft in doing finely
A multitude of unromantic things.

The heroism of thy true endeavour
Shall gild the common-place of common days,
And God Himself shall guard thy work for ever,
And crown it with eternity of praise.

O LOVE, O LOVE, HOW LONG?

THE tree that yearns with drooping crest
O'er some deep river's tranquil breast
At length grows downward, and is blest—
    O Love, O Love, how long?

Belated birds at set of sun
Go sailing homeward one by one,
For sweets are earned when toil is done—
    O Love, O Love, how long?

The creeper through the tangled maze
Of brushwood following lightless ways
Shall some day reach the unclouded rays—
    O Love, O Love, how long?

The barque that strains with groaning mast
Though troubled seas and skies o'ercast
Shall sight the wished-for port at last—
    O Love, O Love, how long?

The traveller spent by many a mile
Plods grimly on, yet knows the while
That all will end in one fond smile—
    O Love, O Love, how long?

The hope of pleasure softens pain,
And if by suffering men attain,
A present loss is future gain—
    O Love, O Love, how long?

SONG

O CAREFUL out of measure
To fence your lovely treasure
With prudence unavailing
    From what must surely be,
How quick you scent a danger
From any comely stranger
Who leans upon a railing,
    Or lurks beneath a tree !

Then close the blind demurely,
And lock the door securely,
And lest a fraud should happen,
    Be watchful of the key ;
But O you may be certain
That Love will draw the curtain,
And throw the casement open,
    And look abroad to see.

And if the Fates be kindly,
And manage not too blindly,
Young Love will hatch a treason,
    And struggle to be free ;
And though you may not guess it,
Nor any sign confess it,
The lips you think in prison
    Will be kissing on the lea.

LOVE'S DELAY

They sat—they two—upon the cliff together,
  And watched the moonlight dance along the swell,
Till broke upon their pleasance 'mid the heather
  The midnight warning of the village bell.

"Good night, my love," he said; "we pass the measure
  Of blessing which in one day's lap can lie;
To linger later were to weary Pleasure,
  And draw some brightness from Tomorrow's eye."

They rose, and gave a last fond look at ocean,
  And then another, and again one more,
And lingering thus, at every homeward motion
  They noted some delight unseen before.

So waned the Night; and when young Morn upstarted
  And quenched pale Luna's lamp with ruddier glare,
He found them parting yet, and yet unparted,—
  Still pledged to move, and still love-anchored there.

DON'T YOU THINK—?

Don't you think that if a torrent,
  Rushing on its seaward way,
Found a jewel lying softly
  On its bed of primal clay,
It would seize and bear it onward,
  Smiling with a smile of spray?

Don't you think that any zephyr
  With a spirit of its own,
If it met a little cloudlet
  Idling where no wind had blown,
Quick would clasp it,—quite refusing
  Any more to fly alone?

Don't you think that Love the Torrent,
  Love the Zephyr, whereso'er
It shall meet a soul untrammelled,
  Happy, free, and debonair,
Can and will and must embrace it,
  All eternity to share?

THE PAGE

I

" Room for Her Highness, ladies gay !
Gentlemen-ushers, clear the way !"
A flourish of trumpets makes known to all
That Madame de Bourbon will open the ball.

With stately mien, and paces slow,
Up to the daïs the courtiers go,
But what is the creature that strives amain
To carry the weight of the royal train ?

Is it an imp in human shape,
Or a stunted kind of hairless ape ?
Surely it beggars the best of eyes
To follow a form in such disguise.

Look at him well, and then confess
That if, as they say, the art of dress
Is the power to hide, there can't be room
For any reform in yon costume.

A tunic of red with golden lace,
A collar that seems to fence his face,
A velvet pelisse of sapphire blue
And a monster rosette on either shoe ;

Fettered with ribands ; condemned to wear
A wig of somebody else's hair,
A necklace of gems as large as eggs,
And a sword that is always between his legs ;

More than monkey, and less than man—
There never was seen, since Time began,
Such a queer grotesque, I dare engage,
As Madame de Bourbon's youngest page.

II

The ball is over: with aching head
The poor little page steals off to bed,
And stripped of the velvet and gold brocade
Is simply the boy that God has made.

Sleep sound, tired fellow! Sweet dreams be yours
Of the château away on the Gascon moors;
Of the father, so stern and yet so true,
Of the mother whose prayers are all for you;

Of the dear little Marie you long to kiss,
And the sturdy limbs of young Narcisse;
Of Léon the hound, polite and tame,
But ever agog for sport or game;

Of Jacquot the pony you once could ride
At your own free will o'er the country-side;—
Till the sun looks in through the window-pane,
And you lose your boyhood over again.

COLORES

A MOAN AFTER MOON-SET

*A parody of Mr. Swinburne's style as exemplified
in " Dolores "*

O THOU that art sanguine and subtle,
　　With fingers so wicked and white,
And eyes that are black as a cuttle,
　　And brows that are blue as a blight.
O terriblest torture invented !
　　O purplest passion intense !
(Have you heard of a poet demented,
　　Benign Common-sense ?)

O love that is redder than roses !
　　O hate that is whiter than snow !
That blinkedly blindedly blazes,
　　When black-blooded blast-blisses blow ;
Desert us, disdain us, O never !
　　Still fashion our fatuous fate ;
O lick us and kick us for ever,
　　Red love and white hate !

Let thy crying out-crimson the poppy,
　　Thy yellings out-yellow the moon
All gilt with the gold of her copy
　　While thy moanings are simply maroon ;
Let the robe of thy redness be rounded,
　　And the doom of desire be dense ;
(Let the meaning of this be expounded,
　　Say I, Common-sense.)

By the foam and the froth and the flashes,
   The flashes, the froth and the foam,
By the crag-cradled craving and crashes
   Through globulous glimmering gloom,
By the red, by the redder, the reddest,
   The greenest, the greener, the green,
By the folly that feeds where thou feddest,
   And licks thy plate clean.

By the fin-smashing fists that have smitten
   The bruises that blacken and bud,
By the tawny-tailed cur that has bitten
   When the thong has come down with a thud,
By all that is cruel and crimson,
   By all that is mean and immense,
(In a word, by the horrors he hymns on,
   Benign Common-sense.)

Who shall say whether red is ecstatic,
   Or green a more furious hue?
Must it always remain problematic
   Whether passion is purple or blue?
Sea-serpents sequestered in sadness,
   That satiate sorrow with salt,
O read us this riddle of madness,
   Since *we* are at fault!

So the saffron shall simulate sable,
   The bluest and blackest shall blend,
All the bases shall build them a Babel,
   Red, blue, green,—and so on to the end.
(Ye bards that make Bedlam your model,
   Remove your absurdities hence!
Come down and redeem us from twaddle,
   Benign Common-sense!)

Oxford, 1876.

LOOKING BACK

We walked in June thro' garden beds
    Made bright with every flower that blows,
And high above their dewy heads
    A rose, and yet again a rose.

They bent to meet you from the stem,
    You touched their petals as we passed;
(No gentler hand could fall on them)
    "Sweet things," you murmured,—"while they last.

And I on cheerful thoughts intent:
    "How well they grace their tiny room!
Without a struggle yielding scent,
    Without an effort spreading bloom.

And why should *we* so toil to please,
    When simple truth is all in all?
What can we compass more than these?"
    You smiled and said, "But ah, they fall!"

November glooms are round us now,
    I sit within and dream of you—
Your look, your smile, your thoughtful brow,
    Your pensive word—alas, 'twas true!

The fairest thing makes shortest stay,
    The sweetest thing the soonest goes;
Shed were the rose's leaves to-day,
    And you—you went before the rose!

1884.

"LORD, AND WHAT SHALL THIS MAN DO?"

O LORD, Thy wisdom leads us best
  To where our duties lie ;
Thou giv'st without perturbing quest
  The light to find them by.

And if our hearts would fain be told,
  For self or dearest friend,
What doom in God's high book is scrolled,
  What work His love shall send ;

Let this thought be for comfort—not
  To Peter, not to John,
Was told the fulness of the lot
  That years were leading on.

To one a glimpse was given, no more,
  In dark prophetic show,—
To one not then imperious, nor
  Importunate to know.

And he to whom a little while
  Would bring that vision fair,
Heard not as yet of Patmos' Isle,
  And what should greet him there.

But feed My sheep, the Saviour said,
  Disciple, follow Me !
In My pure footsteps meekly tread,—
  The rest is not for thee !

And so to us the warning comes,
  When faith is tossed at sea,—
The simple word of trust which sums
  True Love's philosophy.

Hereafter lies with God—enough !
  Our path begins from here ;
Our next step, be it smooth or rough,
  Our Master maketh clear.

No hearts with sacred love elate,
  Whose lamps are burning still,
Can linger in such vexed estate
  As not to know His will.

Our shades shall never lie so deep,
  Our landscape grow so dim,
That we need fail to feed His sheep,
  Or cease from following Him.

CLASS-MAKING

THERE is a habit very common among boys, and, I am afraid, among grown-up people too, of grouping their fellows into artificial classes, and calling them by a common title or name. At school it is "the boys who don't play games," "the boys who work hard at their books," "the boys whose dress is not always of the tidiest or newest," and so on. Each of these classes is known by some name,—some dry, cold, descriptive, and probably contemptuous title. After school the classes will be different, but the principle of division remains the same. It is always a lumping together of persons who have an outward prominent characteristic in common, and a labelling of them as one might label a row of identical insects in a cabinet.

"Well," you say, "and is it not a very convenient plan? What objection can you bring against it?"

My friends, I can bring a most serious objection,— the objection that it is not a true plan, and therefore not a fair plan.

1. In the first place, it is not *true*. You cannot classify human beings in such a simple way, if you wish your classification to be accurate. One or two prominent features are not enough to go by; and very often

NOTE.—This is one of "Six Addresses to Senior Boys in a Public School" (*v.* Memoir p. 61).

M

the more conspicuous they seem, the less significant they really are for any purpose of useful classification. It is the sure mark of an ignorant and superficial observer to think otherwise.

Let me illustrate what I mean.

You have all heard of Linnæus, the great Swedish botanist, and some of you perhaps may be acquainted with what is called the "Linnæan system" of arranging plants. Linnæus, you know, was the father of modern botany. It was he who made the first successful attempt to distinguish the myriad flowers which carpet the earth, and to gather them into classes and families. And how did he go to work? He looked at a great variety of blossoms, and he saw that one conspicuous difference between them lay in the number of their stamens. Some had many stamens; some had few. Some had twenty or more; some had only one. And he said, "I will arrange my plants according to this feature. There shall be a class of one-stamen plants, like the Red Valerian; a class of two-stamen plants, like the Veronica; a class of three-stamen plants, like the Crocus; and so on." It was probably the best arrangement he could make with the very limited knowledge at his disposal.

But what happened when knowledge grew wider,— when botanists had discovered many new plants, and many new things about the plants that were old? Why, simply this. The arrangement of Linnæus fell to the ground. It was not merely altered. It was superseded. Scientific men examined the organs of plants with microscopes, and they found that the number of stamens is not nearly so important a matter as Linnæus fancied. They found that a flower with one stamen may be own-brother to a flower with six stamens, and only fiftieth cousin to a flower with no more stamens than itself. And the modern arrangement ("Natural" arrangement, as it is called), of plants, which has succeeded the rough-and-ready fallacious Linnæan system, is so complex—it depends upon so many different features (some very minute and barely visible) in the plant, that if I were to talk about it for an hour, you might not be much wiser than when I began.

You see my point. If it be thus difficult to classify plants—organisms low down in the scale of nature—how can it be easy to classify men—the most highly organised of created things? If by taking a few conspicuous parts of a flower, and making them the signposts of a system, we can arrive at such misleading, such fallacious results, what do you suppose will be the outcome of the same blind philosophy when applied to the analysis of human motives and human character?

Now let us descend from theory to practice. You tell me, for instance, that boys who show themselves indifferent players of football and cricket ought, in your opinion, to be—well, condemned. They are, you say, x and y and z, and many other objectionable things. In short, you put them all together into a single class, and label them with an ugly name. Is that an arrangement in accord with natural truth? Will it bear enquiry? Will it, to use a common phrase, hold water? I am sure it will not.

Consider for a moment how it grew up. Once upon a time (you may fix the epoch when you will) there were certain lads—call them A, B, C,—who fancied that loafing and smoking, and getting into mischief was "more fun" than any pastime to be found in the playing-field. You noticed these fellows. You pitied them. You condemned them. You called them x, y, z. And you did well. It was a just and healthy condemnation. But unfortunately you did not stop at this point.

There were certain other lads—call them D, E, F,—
lads of good disposition, but of nervous temperament,
or bookish taste, or conscious of limbs set awkwardly in
their sockets,—who therefore joined in your games no
oftener and no more heartily than rule or custom
obliged; and you, in the shallowness of your heart,
looked with indignant eyes upon these, even as you
looked upon the former set. Practically you swept
D, E, F, into same class with A, B, C, and you called
them x, y, z. Was it well done? I think not.

Take another example. There are boys in every
school who study hard, win dozens of prizes, and stand
always at the head of the Form. "I don't like such
fellows," you say; "they are selfish; they are mean;
they care nothing for the corporate welfare; they look
only to their own interest; they want to seize more
than their share of honours and distinctions, and they
go about the business in a underhand way." Now *why*
do you say this? Are you the exponents of a baseless
grudge, or the victims of an ill-natured delusion? No,
not altogether. There is a modicum of truth in your
indictment,—a small space of solid earth on which the
feet of your logic may rest. As long as the competitive
system prevails in matters educational, so long will a
few lads suffer deterioration of the kind you hint
at. They will become self-centred and self-engrossed.
They will take a narrow view of what the school can
give to the scholar. They will ignore entirely what
the scholar should give back to the school. Good-
fellowship, public spirit, united effort for a common
cause,—these things are above and beyond them.
Only what is "paying" and personal has any charm for
their souls. Such lads exist; and neither industry nor
talent can make them estimable persons.

But *all* boys who study hard and win prizes are not

of this sort. Very far from it indeed. Some boys stand high in class, because their mental power is such that they could not easily stand anywhere else. Others owe distinction to an honest, single-hearted endeavour to do their duty in the class-room as they would do it in the playing-field. Others again have a conscious and laudable desire to get all the help that teachers can give them towards fulfilling the noblest of aims—"to be a good soldier and servant of Jesus Christ." Nothing can be alleged against the industrious boy, whose industry is of the right—which I believe, on the whole, to be the ordinary—type. Schools exist, remember, for the purpose of imparting education. And though book-learning is only one element in a perfect education, in the education which great schools do their best to give,—it is never-the-less by far the most *important* element. And therefore you sin against the fitness of things, as well as against natural truth, if by hasty and inconsiderate classification you impose a stigma on the whole body of hard-working boys.

Yet again. There are lads in every school whose dress and general appearance is not of the neatest. You have no difficulty in picking them out, because at the present day slovenliness is far from being the general characteristic of the school-boy. And against these also you take up your parable. "Lazy underbred good-for-nothing fellows," you call them, "without any proper feeling of what is due to themselves, to their school, or to the gentlemen who belong to it. Can any smartness, or brightness, or cleverness," you ask, "come out of such unkempt tabernacles?" Well, the plain truth is—they can. If I were to go through the list of great men who are known to have neglected their raiment from infancy to old age, I should weary your patience almost as much as if I expounded the

Natural System of classifying plants. It may be disagreeable to reflect that fine characters are so often unmethodical, ill-balanced, and destitute of care for the details of practical life. But we must accept genius as we find it, and not seek to deny its place or power, because it appears to be weak in the science of dress.

"Quite so," you say, "but suppose our slovenly boys are *not* geniuses ; what then ?" Then judge them with a righteous, that is, a discriminating judgment. If they have not "the defect of their qualities," they may be the victims of a bad bringing up, they may have inherited an incurable carelessness from generations of untidy ancestors, or their want of lustre at school may be due in part to a want of money at home. This last consideration should, I think, make us doubly cautious how we impute moral blame for reasons of dress. And yet—mark me—I do not deny for a moment that *some* lads deserve the heaviest censure you can deal out to them. These by all means take in hand for the speedier reformation of their manners. Put them into the class of the criminal, that they may presently emerge into the class of the penitent, and so pass to the great body of the cleansed. Only be watchful that you include in the purging process no victims of inheritance or misfortune or destiny, who, in the eyes of the great Judge of all men, might more properly do execution upon *you*.

2. I have shown the untruthfulness of indiscriminate class-making, and I could not help showing something of its unfairness at the same time. But I want you to consider this latter point more at large.

The unfairness which I have spoken of already consists in arguing from the boy to the class. It is of a constructive unfairness. You say—"So-and-so is of such-and-such a character, and therefore he belongs to such-and-such a class." But there is also a deductive unfairness. It consists in arguing from the class to the boy. You say—"So-and-so belongs to such-and-such a class, and therefore he must be of such-and-such a character."

Now if the classification of human beings were accurate, exhaustive, unerring, there would be no unfairness in drawing a conclusion of this sort. But, as a matter of fact, it is not more accurate or exhaustive or unerring than was the Linnæan classification of plants; and you can easily understand how fallacious (beyond the narrowest area) would be any conclusions drawn from *that*. It would never do to argue about the shape of a blossom from the number of its stamens. Still less could you form an idea of the whole plant— its roots, its stem, its leaves, its months of flowering, or the soil it would choose to live in. The primrose, the forget-me-not, the buckthorn, the chickweed, the convolvulus, and the elm, all have five stamens; all belong to the same Linnæan class *Pentandria*. Clearly, if you knew the chickweed and did not know the primrose, and then, relying on the Linnæan system, you concluded that the primrose is *like* the chickweed, you would do a great injustice to the primrose; but not a greater injustice than you may do to individual human beings by regarding them as types of some class which really has nothing typical about it.

When you are told that a schoolfellow belongs to a section of the school which you hold in light esteem, beware how you pour upon him the vials of your scorn. There *may* be sound reason for ranking him where public opinion dictates; but on the other hand, there may be no reason at all which a fair judgment could recognise. You cannot tell without a personal acquaintance with the boy. Gain this, and you will be

qualified to judge. Perhaps the very lad you were
warned against may become the friend you were
craving for; and you will smile after many days to
think how ill-founded was your initial estimate—your
estimate *before you knew*.

Now look at the matter from another side. What
do you suppose are the feelings of the boy himself,
who has been wrongly included in a contemptible
class? Is it possible that he should feel happy, or
even healthy, if a sound mind be part of health?
The first ingredient in a healthy happiness is self-
respect; and how can any one respect himself when
nobody else respects him? The boy has lost the good
esteem of his fellows, and he has lost it, remember,
almost, if not quite, beyond retrieval. It is the hardest
thing in the world to get rid of a stigma once attached.
The label which public opinion affixes to you when you
enter a school, is the label which you will probably bear
as long as you remain in it. Everybody knows this.
The boy knows it best of all. " I have been condemned unheard," he says, " and there is no appeal
from the verdict. I can never be popular, or influential,
or trusted. Nobody cares for me. Nobody loves me.
People have given me a bad name, and it will stick to
me till the end." I ask you again, if any boy so
weighted can enjoy happiness or moral health. And I
appeal to you as high-minded gentlemen to be as
scrupulously fair in your judgments as you are, I trust,
in the other relations of corporate life.

Let me conclude with a practical suggestion. We
can not only minimise the evils of an imperfect system
which we find ready-made to our hand, but we can
construct a better system, above it and beyond it and
beneath it, to take its place in our own hearts, and
some day perhaps in the world at large. That will be

a system grounded on essentials, and not on outside show, a system which regards motive and temper and habitual bias, as more important than any single characteristic of the conduct which can be seen. The class-names in that system will be brief but significant: the Honest, the Loving, the Brave, the Faithful, the Pure; the Mean, the Envious, the Selfish, the Time-serving, and the Corrupt. From such divisions no mistake can arise; for they are rooted and grounded in eternal truth. Tell me that a man is pre-eminently honest or pre-eminently brave, and I know a great deal about him beyond the possibility of error. It is as though you told me that some new plant belongs to the Natural Family of the *Crucifers* or of the *Compositæ*, and straightway I infer all the leading details of its character and constitution. Few things are more useful than a plan of social divisions broadly and spiritually based; few more pernicious than one which has no basis but the casual observation of the unreflecting crowd.

If you desire (as I hope you do) to see this matter in the highest and purest light vouchsafed to us, look at the divine history of our Blessed Lord. Zacchæus was not divided from Him, nor was Levi, nor was Mary Magdalene, by the barriers which the men of that day had set up. He acknowledged no bar, He raised no bar, where none existed in the counsels of the Almighty. And yet he came to divide, as truly as He came to knit together. You find, in His Gospel, the merciful, the peace-makers, the pure in heart, set over against and contrasted with the "hypocrites" who shall receive "greater damnation." You find "the children of this world" sharply distinguished from "the children of light." You find "the tares" spoken of, and you find "the wheat."

Be it ours to follow with reverent humility in the steps of the Master. Let us make no divisions which He would not approve,—set up no barriers which His love would immediately break down. When we divide, as divide we sometimes must, let it be in the spirit of Him who bade us "judge righteous judgment" not based on external show. For while man—inconsiderate man—"looketh on the outward appearance, the Lord looketh on the heart."

A CRITICAL ESTIMATE

A CRITICAL ESTIMATE

BY JOHN ADDINGTON SYMONDS

I

NOT long ago, a writer in *The Artist* quoted some lines of remarkable dignity and beauty by E. C. L. I felt that here was a poet unknown to me; for the verses had that peculiar quality which belongs alone to genuine inspiration. By the kindness of the editor of *The Artist* I obtained a copy of the book from which the extracts had been made. It is a thin volume, entitled " Echoes from Theocritus, and Other Sonnets." By Edward Cracroft Lefroy. London : Elliot Stock, 1885. The first thirty Sonnets are composed on themes suggested by the Syracusan idyllist. Of miscellaneous sonnets there are seventy. So, whether by accident or intention, the poet rests his fame upon a century of sonnets, by far the most important of these being the seventy which do not give their title to the book.

Together with this volume came the sad intelligence that Edward Lefroy died last summer after a tedious illness. In reply to inquiries, I learned, through the courtesy of one of his best and oldest friends, that he

NOTE.—Most of the Sonnets cited by Symonds are here omitted for economy of space. The reader is referred to the collection (pp. 95–129).

was educated at Blackheath Proprietary School and at Keble College, Oxford. In 1878 he took orders. His sonnets originally appeared in four small paper-covered pamphlets, severally entitled " Echoes from Theocritus," " Cytisus and Galingale," the " Windows of the Church," and " Sketches and Studies." They were published at Blackheath by H. Burnside, bookseller, between the years 1883 and 1884, and attracted comparatively little notice. In 1885 the same sonnets were collected under the title and description I have given above. Few of our well-known literary critics, with the exception of Mr. Andrew Lang and Mr. William Sharp, took notice of them and discerned their merit. Later on, Mr. Lefroy gave a volume of sermons to the public, and in 1885 he printed a very characteristic collection of " Addresses to Senior School Boys." He was thirty-six years of age when he died.

Though Mr. Lefroy worked as a parish clergyman both at Truro and Lambeth with the late and the present * Archbishops of Canterbury, he suffered from chronic physical weakness of a distressing nature. As early as the year 1882, he learned from the best medical authority that his heart was seriously affected, and that he could not expect length of life. The pains and wearinesses of illness he bore with what a critic, writing in the *Academy*, well described as " breezy healthfulness of thought and feeling." Combining in a singular measure Hellenic cheerfulness with Christian faith and patience, he was able to await death with a spiritual serenity sweeter than the steadfastness of Stoical endurance. In one of his diaries he wrote : " The world contains, even for an invalid like me, a multitude of beautiful and inspiring things I

* This was written in March 1892 (ED.).

have always tried to live a broad life. It has been my pleasure to sympathise with all sorts and conditions of men in their labours and their recreations. Art, nature, and youth have yielded to me 'the harvest of a quiet eye.' It would be affectation to pretend that I am weary of existence .... but I have faith enough in my Lord to follow Him willingly where he has gone before." His sympathy with youthful strength and beauty, his keen interest in boyish games and the athletic sports of young men, seem to have kept his nature always fresh and wholesome. These qualities were connected in a remarkable way with Hellenic instincts and an almost pagan delight in nature. But Lefroy's temperament assimilated from the Christian and the Greek ideals only what is really admirable in both : discarding the asceticism of the one and the sensuousness of the 'other. The twofold elements in him were kindly mixed and blended in a rare beauty and purity of manliness. Writing to a friend about his Theocritean sonnets, he says that he composed them in order to relax his mind. "To a man occupied in sermon-writing and parochial visitation it is intellectual change of air to go back in thought to a pre-Christian age : and I confess that I have never been able to emancipate myself (as most clergymen do) from the classical bonds which schoolmasters and college tutors for so many years did their best to weave around me. And then I have such an intense sympathy with the joys and griefs, hopes and fears, passions and actions of 'the young life' that I find myself in closer affinity to Greek feeling than most people would. At the same time I should be sorry to help on that Hellenic revival which some Oxford teachers desire." At another time he writes : "I find the school of Keats more congenial to my 'natural man' than the school of Keble. And

in my more truthful moments the temper of Sophocles
seems more akin to mine than the temper of Thomas à
Kempis, though the ' Imitatio ' is seldom far from my
hand.   I mean to struggle on to a less perishable
standpoint, and hope (D.V.) to diminish the frequency
of my lapses into Hellenism."

II

There is a strong personal accent in all Lefroy wrote ;
the "breezy healthfulness of thought and feeling"
which his reviewer noted ; the untainted Hellenism
broadening and clarifying Christian virtues, which I
have attempted to describe.

This attitude of mind is sufficiently well set forth in
the last sonnet of the series, entitled "An Apology"
(No. lxx).

Some of Lefroy's finest work is done in the key
suggested by this sonnet.   He felt that life itself is
more than literature : the real poems are not what we
sing, but what we feel and see.   This thought, which is
indeed the base-note of all Walt Whitman's theories
upon Art, is admirably rendered in "From Any Poet"
(No. xxxvii).

Feeling this, Lefroy felt, like Alfred de Musset, that
the poet's true applause is praise bestowed upon him
by the young :

> O hearts of youth, so brightly, frankly true,
> To gods and bards alike your praise is dear ;
> Though wreaths from adult hands be all unseized,
> Our crowns are crowns indeed if thrown by you.

These lines, from a sonnet entitled "A Story of
Aurelius" (No. xxxviii), suffer by their severance from
the rest of the poem.   It may be said, indeed, in passing, that, spontaneous and unstudied as his work

appears, Lefroy had a fine sense of unity. None of his pieces, to my mind, can be rightly estimated, except in their total effect. As an illustration of this, take "Bill : A Portrait" (No. xxxvi).

The grace of this composition is almost rustic, the music like to that of some old ditty piped by shepherds in the shade. The subrisive irony, the touch of humour, the quiet sympathy with nature's and fortune's gilded darling, give it a peculiar raciness. But after all is said, it leaves a melody afloat upon the brain, a savour on the mental palate. Only lines four and five seem to interrupt the rhythm by sibilants and a certain poverty of phrase—as though (which was perhaps the case) two separate compositions had been patched together.

A companion portrait, this time of a maiden, may be placed beside it—"Flora " (No. xxxv).

In all these sonnets there are charming single lines :—

How near of kin we are to springing flowers.

Of children, in another place, he says :—

To you the glory and to us the debt.

And again, in yet another sonnet :—

We press and strive and toil from morn till eve ;
From eve to morn our waking thoughts are grim.
Were children silent, we should half believe
That joy was dead—its lamp would burn so dim.

This special sympathy with what he called "the young life " finds noble expression in four sonnets dedicated to the sports of boyhood—"A Football Player" (No. xxvii), "A Cricket Bowler " (No. xxviii), and "Before the Race " (No. xxix).

Very finely conceived and splendidly expressed is the fourth of these athletic sonnets, which connects æsthetic

N

impressions with underlying moral ideas.   "A Palæstral Study " (No. xxxi) :—

> The curves of beauty are not softly wrought :
> These quivering limbs by strong hid muscles held
> In attitudes of wonder, and compelled
> Through shapes more sinuous than a sculptor's thought,
> Tell of dull matter splendidly distraught,
> Whisper of mutinies divinely quelled—
> Weak indolence of flesh, that long rebelled,
> The spirit's domination bravely taught.
> And all man's loveliest works are cut with pain.
> Beneath the perfect art we know the strain,
> Intense, defined, how deep soe'er it lies.
> From each high masterpiece our souls refrain,
> Not tired of gazing, but with stretchèd eyes
> Made hot by radiant flames of sacrifice.

I think it will be felt, from these examples, that in Lefroy's now almost forgotten work a true poet drew authentic inspiration from the beautiful things which lie nearest to the artist's vision in the life of frank and simple human beings.   His sonnets rank high in that region of Art which I have elsewhere called "democratic."   The sensibility to subjects of this sort may be frequent among us ; but the power of seizing on their essence, the faculty for lifting them into the æsthetic region without marring their wilding charm, are rare. For this reason, because just here seems to lie his originality, I have dwelt upon this group of poems. Their neo-Hellenism is so pure and modern, their feeling for physical beauty and strength is so devoid of sensuality, their tone is so right and yet so warmly sympathetic, that many readers will be grateful to a singer, distinguished by rare personal originality, who touched common and even carnal things with such distinction.   I might enforce this argument by quoting The New Cricket Ground," " Childhood and Youth,"

"In the Cloisters, Winchester College." But, as the Greeks said, the half is more than the whole.

III

The thirty "Echoes from Theocritus" are all penetrated with that purged Hellenic sentiment which was the note of Lefroy's genius. They are exquisite cameos in miniature carved upon fragments broken from the idylls ; nor do I disagree with a critic who said, when they first appeared, that "rarely has the great pastoral poet been so freely transmuted without loss of his spell." Nevertheless, these sonnets have not the same personal interest, nor, in my opinion, the same artistic importance, as others in which the poet's fancy dealt more at large with themes suggested to him by his study of the Greek past. Take for instance : "Something Lost " (No. xviii).

Here we feel that Lefroy (like Wordsworth when he yearned for Triton rising in authentic vision from the sea) had his soul lodged in Hellas. Of how many English poets may not this be said ? "Come back, ye wandering Muses, come back home !" Landor was right. The home of the imagination of the artist is in Greece. Gray, Keats, Shelley, even Byron, Landor, Wordsworth, even Matthew Arnold, all the great and good poets who have passed away from us, signified this truth in one way or in another, each according to his quality. It was the distinction of Lefroy that he "came back home " with a peculiarly fresh and child-like perception of its charm. Seeking to define his touch upon Hellenic things, I find only a barren and scholastic formula : he had a spiritual apperception of sensuous beauty. The strong, clear music which throbbed so piercingly, so passionately, round the Isles of Greece, reached his sense attenuated and refined— like the notes of the Alpine horn, after ascending and tingling through a thousand feet of woods and water- falls and precipices. Read the echo of it in his sonnet, " On the Beach in November " (No. xvii).

How he could convey a single Greek suggestion into the body of an English poem may be exemplified by " A Thought from Pindar " (No. xxxix).

The contrast between the powers of two rival arts, sculpture and poetry, to confer immortal fame upon some noble agent in the world's drama, has been well conceived and forcibly presented.

Like all poets who have confined their practice mainly to contemplative and meditative forms of verse, Lefroy reflected on the nature of art. That he was not in theory " the idle singer of an idle day " may be gathered from a sonnet entitled " Art that Endures " (No. lxviii) :—

> Marble of Paros, bronze that will not rust,
> Onyx or agate—sculptor, choose thy block !
> Not clay nor wax nor perishable stock
> Of earthy stones can yield a virile bust
> Keen-edged against the centuries. Strive thou must
> In molten brass or adamantine rock
> To carve the strenuous shape which shall not mock
> Thy faith by crumbling dust upon thy dust.
> Poet, the warning comes not less to thee !
> Match well thy metres with a strong design.
> Let noble themes find nervous utterance.   Flee
> The frail conceit, the weak mellifluous line.
> High thoughts, hard forms, toil, rigour—these be thine
> And steadfast hopes of immortality.

With this lofty conception of the spirit in which the artist should approach his task, Lefroy did not ex- aggerate his own capacity as poet or seek to exalt his

function. A sonnet called "The Torch Bearer" (No.
lxvi) expresses, in a charming metaphor, the thought
that poetry is but the soul's light cast upon the world
for other souls to see by.

In another place (No. i) he disclaims his right or
duty to attack the higher paths of poesy, saying of his
Muse :—

> She hath no mind for "freaks upon the fells,"
> No wish to hear the storm-wind rattling by :
> She loves her cowslips more than immortelles,
> Her garden-closes than the abysmal sky :
> In a green dale her chosen sweetheart dwells :
> The mountain-height she must not, dare not, try.

That sense of inadequacy which every modest worker
feels from time to time, when he compares "this man's
art or that man's scope" with his own performance,
and the reaction from its benumbing oppression under
the influence of healthier reflection, are expressed with
delightful spontaneity in "Two Thoughts" (No.
xliii) :—

> When I reflect how small a space I fill
> In this great teeming world of labourers,
> How little I can do with strongest will,
> How marred that little by most hateful blurs,—
> The fancy overwhelms me, and deters
> My soul from putting forth so poor a skill :
> Let me be counted with those worshippers
> Who lie before God's altar and are still.
> But then I think (for healthier moments come),
> This power of will, this natural force of hand,—
> What do they mean, if working be not wise ?
> Forbear to weigh thy work, O Soul ! Arise,
> And join thee to that nobler, sturdier band
> Whose worship is not idle, fruitless, dumb.

IV

It was not to be expected that a man who vibrated so deeply and truly to the beauty of the world and to the loveliness of "the young life," and who was himself condemned to life-long sickness with no prospect but the grave upon this planet, should not have left some utterances upon the problems of death and thwarted vitality. It must be remembered, however, that Lefroy was a believing Christian, and for him the tomb was, therefore, but a doorway opened into regions of eternal life. It is highly characteristic of the man that, in his poetry, he made no vulgar appeal to the principles of his religious creed, but remained within the region of that Christianised Stoicism I have attempted to define. We feel this strongly in the sonnets "To an Invalid" (No. liv), "On Reading a Poet's Life" (No. lix), and "The Dying Prince" (No. xlvii). All of these, for their intrinsic merits, are worthy of citation. But space fails; and I would fain excite some curiosity for lovely things to be discovered by the reader when a full edition of Lefroy's *Remains* appears. I shall, therefore, content myself with the transcription of the following most original poem upon the old theme of "Quem Di Diligunt" (No. lvii) :—

O kiss the almond-blossom on the rod !
A thing has gone from us that could not stay.
At least our sad eyes shall not see one day
All baseness treading where all beauty trod.
O kiss the almond-blossom on the rod !
For this our budding Hope is caught away
From growth that is not other than decay
To bloom eternal in the halls of God.
And though of subtler grace we saw no sign,
No glimmer from the yet unrisen star,—

Full-orbed he broke upon the choir divine,
Saint among saints beyond the golden bar,
Round whose pale brows new lights of glory shine—
The aureoles that were not and that are.

The artistic value of Lefroy's work is great. That first attracted me to him, before I knew what kind of man I was to meet with in the poet. Now that I have learned to appreciate his life-philosophy, it seems to me that this is even more noteworthy than his verse. We are all of us engaged, in some way or another, with the problem of co-ordinating the Hellenic and Christian ideals, or, what is much the same thing, of adapting Christian traditions to the governing conceptions of a scientific age. Lefroy proved that it is possible to combine religious faith with frank delight in natural loveliness, to be a Christian without asceticism, and a Greek without sensuality. I can imagine that this will appear simple to many of my readers. They will exclaim : "We do not need a minor poet like Lefroy to teach that lesson. Has not the problem been solved by thousands ?" Perhaps it has. But there is a specific note, a particular purity, a clarified distinction, in the amalgam offered by Lefroy. What I have called his spiritual apperception of sensuous beauty was the outcome of a rare and exquisite personality. It has the translucent quality of a gem, beryl or jacinth, which turn it to the light and view it from all sides, retains one flawless colour. This simplicity and absolute sincerity of instinct is surely uncommon in our perplexed epoch. To rest for a moment upon the spontaneous and unambitious poetry which flowed from such a nature cannot fail to refresh minds wearied with the storm and stress of modern thought.

Printed by Ballantyne, Hanson & Co
London and Edinburgh

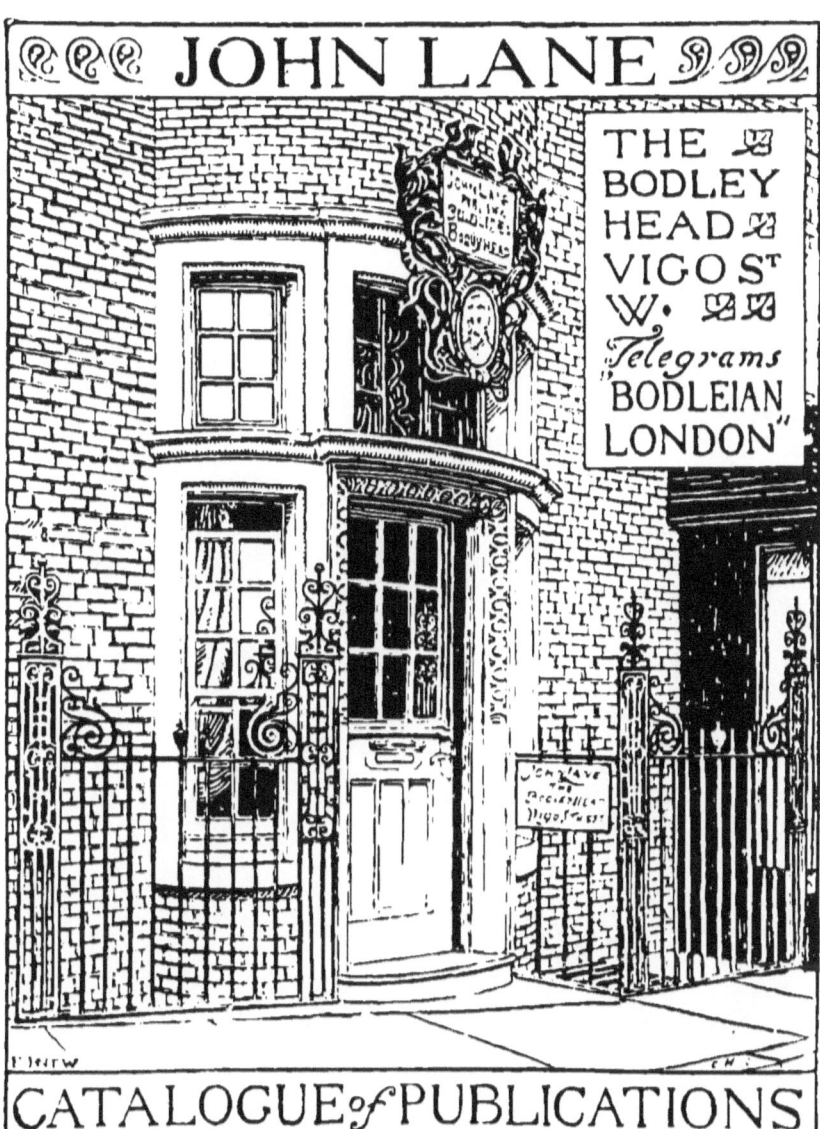

JOHN LANE

THE BODLEY HEAD VIGO St W.

Telegrams "BODLEIAN LONDON"

CATALOGUE of PUBLICATIONS in BELLES LETTRES all at net prices

List of Books

IN

BELLES LETTRES

Published by John Lane

𝔗𝔥𝔢 𝔅𝔬𝔡𝔩𝔢𝔶 𝔥𝔢𝔞𝔡

VIGO STREET, LONDON, W.

Adams (Francis).
ESSAYS IN MODERNITY. Crown 8vo.
5s. net. [*Shortly.*
A CHILD OF THE AGE. (*See* KEY-
NOTES SERIES.)

A. E.
HOMEWARD SONGS BY THE WAY.
Sq. 16mo, wrappers. 1s. 6d. net.
*Transferred to the present Pub-
lisher.* [*Second Edition.*

Aldrich (T. B.)
LATER LYRICS. Sm. Fcap. 8vo.
2s. 6d. net.

Allen (Grant).
THE LOWER SLOPES : A Volume of
Verse. With Title-page and Cover
Design by J. ILLINGWORTH KAY.
Crown 8vo. 5s. net.
THE WOMAN WHO DID. (*See* KEY-
NOTES SERIES.)
THE BRITISH BARBARIANS. (*See*
KEYNOTES SERIES.)

Arcady Library (The).
A Series of Open-Air Books. Edited
by J. S. FLETCHER. With Cover
Designs by PATTEN WILSON.
Each volume crown 8vo. 5s. net.
  I. ROUND ABOUT A BRIGHTON
  COACH OFFICE. By MAUDE
  EGERTON KING. With
  over 30 Illustrations by
  LUCY KEMP-WELCH.
  II. LIFE IN ARCADIA. By J. S.
  FLETCHER. With 20 Illus-
  trations by PATTEN WIL-
  SON.

Arcady Library (The)—*cont.*
  III. SCHOLAR GIPSIES. By JOHN
  BUCHAN. With 7 full-page
  Etchings by D. Y. CAMERON.
  IV. IN THE GARDEN OF PEACE.
  By HELEN MILMAN. With
  24 Illustrations by EDMUND
  H. NEW.
  V. THE HAPPY EXILE. By H.
  D. LOWRY. With 6 Etch-
  ings by E. PHILIP PIMLOTT.
  [*In preparation.*

Beeching (Rev. H. C.).
IN A GARDEN : Poems. With Title-
page designed by ROGER FRY.
Crown 8vo. 5s. net.
ST. AUGUSTINE AT OSTIA. Crown
8vo, wrappers. 1s. net.

Beerbohm (Max).
THE WORKS OF MAX BEERBOHM.
With a Bibliography by JOHN
LANE. Sq. 16mo. 4s. 6d. net.

Benson (Arthur Christopher)
LYRICS. Fcap. 8vo, buckram. 5s.
net.
LORD VYET AND OTHER POEMS.
Fcap. 8vo. 3s. 6d. net.

**Bodley Head Anthologies
(The).**
Edited by ROBERT H. CASE. With
Title-page and Cover Designs by
WALTER WEST. Each volume
crown 8vo. 5s. net.
  I. ENGLISH EPITHALAMIES.
  By ROBERT H. CASE.

Bodley Head Anthologies (The)—*continued.*

II. MUSA PISCATRIX. By JOHN BUCHAN. With 6 Etchings by E. PHILIP PIMLOTT.

III. ENGLISH ELEGIES. By JOHN C. BAILEY.
[*In preparation.*

IV. ENGLISH SATIRES. By CHAS. HILL DICK.
[*In preparation.*

Bridges (Robert).

SUPPRESSED CHAPTERS AND OTHER BOOKISHNESS. Crown 8vo. 3s. 6d. net. [*Second Edition.*

Brotherton (Mary).

ROSEMARY FOR REMEMBRANCE. With Title-page and Cover Design by WALTER WEST. Fcap. 8vo. 3s. 6d. net.

Crackanthorpe (Hubert).

VIGNETTES. A Miniature Journal of Whim and Sentiment. Fcap. 8vo, boards. 2s. 6d. net.

Crane (Walter).

TOY BOOKS. Re-issue, each with new Cover Design and End Papers This LITTLE PIG'S PICTURE BOOK, containing:
I. THIS LITTLE PIG.
II. THE FAIRY SHIP.
III. KING LUCKIEBOY'S PARTY.

The three bound in one volume with a decorative cloth cover, end papers, and a newly written and designed preface and title-page. 3s. 6d. net; separately 9d. net each.

MOTHER HUBBARD'S PICTURE BOOK, containing:
I. MOTHER HUBBARD'S.
II. THE THREE BEARS.
III. THE ABSURD A. B. C.

The three bound in one volume with a decorative cloth cover, end papers, and a newly written and designed preface and title-page. 3s. 6d. net; separately 9d. net each.

Custance (Olive).

OPALS: Poems. Fcap. 8vo. 3s. 6d. net.

Dalmon (C. W.).

SONG FAVOURS. With a Title-page by J. P. DONNE. Sq. 16mo. 3s. 6d. net.

Davidson (John).

PLAYS: An Unhistorical Pastoral; A Romantic Farce; Bruce, a Chronicle Play; Smith, a Tragic Farce; Scaramouch in Naxos, a Pantomime. With a Frontispiece and Cover Design by AUBREY BEARDSLEY. Small 4to. 7s. 6d. net.

FLEET STREET ECLOGUES. Fcap. 8vo, buckram. 4s. 6d. net. [*Third Edition.*

FLEET STREET ECLOGUES. 2nd Series. Fcap. 8vo, buckram. 4s. 6d. net. [*Second Edition.*

A RANDOM ITINERARY AND A BALLAD. With a Frontispiece and Title-page by LAURENCE HOUSMAN. Fcap. 8vo, Irish Linen. 5s. net.

BALLADS AND SONGS. With a Title-page and Cover Design by WALTER WEST. Fcap. 8vo, buckram. 5s. net. [*Fourth Edition.*

NEW BALLADS. Fcap. 8vo, buckram. 4s. 6d. net. [*Second Edition.*

De Tabley (Lord).

POEMS, DRAMATIC AND LYRICAL. By JOHN LEICESTER WARREN (Lord de Tabley). Illustrations and Cover Design by C. S. RICKETTS. Crown 8vo. 7s. 6d. net. [*Third Edition.*

POEMS, DRAMATIC AND LYRICAL. Second Series, uniform in binding with the former volume. Crown 8vo. 5s. net.

Duer (Caroline, and Alice).

POEMS. Fcap. 8vo. 3s. 6d. net.

Egerton (George)

KEYNOTES. (*See* KEYNOTES SERIES.)

DISCORDS. (*See* KEYNOTES SERIES.)

YOUNG OFEG'S DITTIES. A translation from the Swedish of OLA HANSSON. With Title-page and Cover Design by AUBREY BEARDSLEY. Crown 8vo. 3s. 6d. net.

SYMPHONIES. [*In preparation.*

Eglinton (John).
Two Essays on the Remnant.
Post 8vo, wrappers. 1s. 6d net.
Transferred to the present Publisher. [*Second Edition.*

Eve's Library.
Each volume, crown 8vo. 3s. 6d. net.
I. Modern Women. An English rendering of Laura Marholm Hansson's "Das Buch der Frauen" by Hermione Ramsden. Subjects: Sonia Kovalevsky, George Egerton, Eleanora Duse, Amalie Skram, Marie Bashkirtseff, A. Ch. Edgren Lefller.
II. The Ascent of Woman. By Roy Devereux.
III. Marriage Questions in Modern Fiction. By Elizabeth Rachel Chapman.

Fea (Allan).
The Flight of the King : a full, true, and particular account of the escape of His Most Sacred Majesty King Charles II. after the Battle of Worcester, with Sixteen Portraits in Photogravure and nearly 100 other Illustrations. Demy 8vo. 21s. net.

Field (Eugene).
The Love Affairs of a Bibliomaniac. Post 8vo. 3s. 6d. net.

Fletcher (J. S.).
The Wonderful Wapentake. By "A Son of the Soil." With 18 full-page Illustrations by J. A. Symington. Crown 8vo. 5s. 6d. net.
Life in Arcadia. (*See* Arcady Library.)
God's Failures. (*See* Keynotes Series.)
Ballads of Revolt. Sq. 32mo. 2s. 6d. net.

Ford (James L.).
The Literary Shop and Other Tales. Fcap. 8vo. 3s. 6d. net.

Four-and-Sixpenny Novels.
Each volume with Title-page and Cover Design by Patten Wilson. Crown 8vo. 4s. 6d. net.
Galloping Dick. By H. B. Marriott Watson.
The Wood of the Brambles. By Frank Mathew.
The Sacrifice of Fools. By R. Manifold Craig.
A Lawyer's Wife. By Sir Nevill Geary, Bart. [*Second Edition.*
The following are in preparation :
Weighed in the Balance. By Harry Lander.
Glamour. By Meta Orred.
Patience Sparhawk and her Times. By Gertrude Atherton.
The Wise and the Wayward. By G. S. Street.
Middle Greyness. By A. J. Dawson.
The Martyr's Bible. By George Fifth.
A Celibate's Wife. By Herbert Flowerdew.
Max. By Julian Croskey.
The Making of a Prig. By Evelyn Sharp.
The Tree of Life. By Netta Syrett.
Cecilia. By Stanley V. Makower.

Fuller (H. B.).
The Puppet Booth. Twelve Plays. Crown 8vo. 4s. 6d. net.

Gale (Norman).
Orchard Songs. With Title-page and Cover Design by J. Illingworth Kay. Fcap. 8vo, Irish Linen. 5s. net.
Also a Special Edition limited in number on hand-made paper bound in English vellum. £1 1s. net.

Garnett (Richard).
Poems. With Title-page by J. Illingworth Kay. Crown 8vo. 5s. net.
Dante, Petrarch, Camoens, cxxiv Sonnets, rendered in English. With Title-page by Patten Wilson. Crown 8vo. 5s. net.

Gibson (Charles Dana).
Pictures : Eighty-Five Large Cartoons. Oblong Folio. 15s. net.

Gibson (Charles Dana)—
continued.

PICTURES OF PEOPLE. Eighty-Five Large Cartoons. Oblong folio. 15s. net.

Gosse (Edmund).

THE LETTERS OF THOMAS LOVELL BEDDOES. Now first edited. Pott 8vo. 5s. net.
Also 25 copies large paper. 12s. 6d. net

Grahame (Kenneth).

PAGAN PAPERS. With Title-page by AUBREY BEARDSLEY. Fcap. 8vo. 5s. net.
[*Out of Print at present.*
THE GOLDEN AGE. With Cover Design by CHARLES ROBINSON. Crown 8vo. 3s. 6d. net.
[*Fifth Edition.*

Greene (G. A.).

ITALIAN LYRISTS OF TO-DAY. Translations in the original metres from about thirty-five living Italian poets, with bibliographical and biographical notes. Crown 8vo. 5s. net.

Greenwood (Frederick).

IMAGINATION IN DREAMS. Crown 8vo. 5s. net.

Hake (T. Gordon).

A SELECTION FROM HIS POEMS. Edited by Mrs. MEYNELL. With a Portrait after D. G. ROSSETTI, and a Cover Design by GLEESON WHITE. Crown 8vo. 5s. net.

Hayes (Alfred).

THE VALE OF ARDEN AND OTHER POEMS. With a Title-page and a Cover designed by E. H. NEW. Fcap. 8vo. 3s. 6d. net.
Also 25 copies large paper. 15s. net.

Hazlitt (William).

LIBER AMORIS; OR, THE NEW PYGMALION. Edited, with an Introduction, by RICHARD LE GALLIENNE. To which is added an exact transcript of the original MS., Mrs. Hazlitt's Diary in Scotland, and letters never before published. Portrait after BEWICK, and facsimile letters. 400 Copies only. 4to, 364 pp., buckram. 21s. net.

Heinemann (William).

THE FIRST STEP; A Dramatic Moment. Small 4to. 3s. 6d. net.

Hopper (Nora).

BALLAD IN PROSE. With a Title-page and Cover by WALTER WEST. Sq. 16mo. 5s. net.
UNDER QUICKEN BOUGHS. With Title-page designed by PATTEN WILSON, and Cover designed by ELIZABETH NAYLOR. Crown 8vo. 5s. net.

Housman (Clemence).

THE WERE WOLF. With 6 full-page Illustrations, Title-page, and Cover Design by LAURENCE HOUSMAN. Sq. 16mo. 3s. 6d. net.

Housman (Laurence).

GREEN ARRAS: Poems. With 6 Illustrations, Title-page, Cover Design, and End Papers by the Author. Crown 8vo. 5s. net.
GODS AND THEIR MAKERS. Crown 8vo, 3s. 6d. net. [*In preparation.*

Irving (Laurence).

GODEFROI AND YOLANDE: A Play. Sm. 4to. 3s. 6d. net.
[*In preparation.*

James (W. P.)

ROMANTIC PROFESSIONS: A Volume of Essays. With Title-page designed by J. ILLINGWORTH KAY. Crown 8vo. 5s. net.

Johnson (Lionel).

THE ART OF THOMAS HARDY: Six Essays. With Etched Portrait by WM. STRANG, and Bibliography by JOHN LANE. Crown 8vo. 5s. 6d. net. [*Second Edition.*
Also 150 copies, large paper, with proofs of the portrait. £1 1s. net.

Johnson (Pauline).

WHITE WAMPUM: Poems. With a Title-page and Cover Design by E. H. NEW. Crown 8vo. 5s. net.

Johnstone (C. E.).

BALLADS OF BOY AND BEAK. With a Title-page by F. H. TOWNSEND. Sq. 32mo. 2s. net.

Kemble (E. W.)

KEMBLE'S COONS. 30 Drawings of Coloured Children and Southern Scenes. Large 4to. 5s. net.

Keynotes Series.

Each volume with specially-designed Title-page by AUBREY BEARDS-LEY or PATTEN WILSON. Crown 8vo, cloth. 3s. 6d. net.

I. KEYNOTES. By GEORGE EGERTON.
[*Seventh Edition.*

II. THE DANCING FAUN. By FLORENCE FARR.

III. POOR FOLK. Translated from the Russian of F. Dostoievsky by LENA MILMAN. With a Preface by GEORGE MOORE.

IV. A CHILD OF THE AGE. By FRANCIS ADAMS.

V. THE GREAT GOD PAN AND THE INMOST LIGHT. By ARTHUR MACHEN
[*Second Edition.*

VI. DISCORDS. By GEORGE EGERTON.
[*Fifth Edition.*

VII. PRINCE ZALESKI. By M. P. SHIEL.

VIII. THE WOMAN WHO DID. By GRANT ALLEN.
[*Twenty-second Edition.*

IX. WOMEN'S TRAGEDIES. By H. D. LOWRY.

X. GREY ROSES. By HENRY HARLAND.

XI. AT THE FIRST CORNER AND OTHER STORIES. By H. B. MARRIOTT WATSON.

XII. MONOCHROMES. By ELLA D'ARCY.

XIII. AT THE RELTON ARMS. By EVELYN SHARP.

XIV. THE GIRL FROM THE FARM. By GERTRUDE DIX.
[*Second Edition.*

XV. THE MIRROR OF MUSIC. By STANLEY V. MAKOWER.

XVI. YELLOW AND WHITE. By W. CARLTON DAWE.

XVII. THE MOUNTAIN LOVERS. By FIONA MACLEOD.

XVIII. THE WOMAN WHO DIDN'T. By VICTORIA CROSSE
[*Third Edition.*

Keynotes Series—*continued.*

XIX. THE THREE IMPOSTORS. By ARTHUR MACHEN.

XX. NOBODY'S FAULT. By NETTA SYRETT.
[*Second Edition.*

XXI. THE BRITISH BARBARIANS. By GRANT ALLEN.
[*Second Edition.*

XXII. IN HOMESPUN. By E. NESBIT.

XXIII. PLATONIC AFFECTIONS. By JOHN SMITH.

XXIV. NETS FOR THE WIND. By UNA TAYLOR.

XXV. WHERE THE ATLANTIC MEETS THE LAND. By CALDWELL LIPSETT.

XXVI. IN SCARLET AND GREY By FLORENCE HENNIKER. (With THE SPECTRE OF THE REAL by FLORENCE HEN-NIKER and THOMAS HAR-DY.) [*Second Edition.*

XXVII. MARIS STELLA. By MARIE CLOTHILDE BALFOUR.

XXVIII. DAY BOOKS. By MABEL E. WOTTON.

XXIX. SHAPES IN THE FIRE. By M. P. SHIEL.

XXX. UGLY IDOL. By CLAUD NICHOLSON.

The following are in rapid preparation:

XXXI. KAKEMONOS. By W. CARL-TON DAWE.

XXXII. GOD'S FAILURES. By J. S. FLETCHER.

XXXIII. A DELIVERANCE. By ALLAN MONKHOUSE.

XXXIV. MERE SENTIMENT. By A. J. DAWSON.

Lane's Library.

Each volume crown 8vo. 3s. 6d. net.

I. MARCH HARES. By GEORGE FORTH.
[*Second Edition.*

II. THE SENTIMENTAL SEX. By GERTRUDE WARDEN.

III. GOLD. By ANNIE LINDEN.

Lane's Library—*continued.*

The following are in preparation:

IV. BROKEN AWAY. By BEATRICE GRIMSHAW.

V. A MAN FROM THE NORTH. By E. A. BENNETT.

VI. THE DUKE OF LINDEN. By JOSEPH F. CHARLES.

Leather (R. K.).

VERSES. 250 copies. Fcap. 8vo. 3s. net. [*Transferred to the present Publisher.*

Lefroy (Edward Cracroft.)

POEMS. With a Memoir by W. A. GILL, and a reprint of Mr. J. A. SYMONDS' Critical Essay on "Echoes from Theocritus." Cr. 8vo. Photogravure Portrait. 5s. net.

Le Gallienne (Richard).

PROSE FANCIES. With Portrait of the Author by WILSON STEER. Crown 8vo. Purple cloth. 5s. net. [*Fourth Edition.*

Also a limited large paper edition. 12s. 6d. net.

THE BOOK BILLS OF NARCISSUS. An Account rendered by RICHARD LE GALLIENNE. With a Frontispiece. Crown 8vo, purple cloth. 3s. 6d. net. [*Third Edition.*

Also 50 copies on large paper. 8vo. 10s. 6d. net.

ROBERT LOUIS STEVENSON, AN ELEGY, AND OTHER POEMS, MAINLY PERSONAL. With Etched Title-page by D. Y. CAMERON. Crown 8vo, purple cloth. 4s. 6d. net.

Also 75 copies on large paper. 8vo. 12s. 6d. net.

ENGLISH POEMS. Crown 8vo, purple cloth. 4s. 6d. net. [*Fourth Edition, revised.*

GEORGE MEREDITH: Some Characteristics. With a Bibliography (much enlarged) by JOHN LANE, portrait, &c. Crown 8vo, purple cloth. 5s. 6d. net. [*Fourth Edition.*

Le Gallienne (Richard)— *continued.*

THE RELIGION OF A LITERARY MAN. Crown 8vo, purple cloth. 3s. 6d. net. [*Fifth Thousand.*

Also a special rubricated edition on hand-made paper. 8vo. 10s. 6d. net.

RETROSPECTIVE REVIEWS; A LITERARY LOG, 1891–1895. 2 vols. Crown 8vo, purple cloth. 9s. net.

PROSE FANCIES (Second Series). Crown 8vo, Purple cloth. 5s. net.

THE QUEST OF THE GOLDEN GIRL. Crown 8vo. 5s. net.

See also HAZLITT, WALTON and COTTON.

Lowry (H. D.).

MAKE BELIEVE. Illustrated by CHARLES ROBINSON. Crown 8vo, gilt edges or uncut. 5s. net.

WOMEN'S TRAGEDIES. (*See* KEYNOTES SERIES).

THE HAPPY EXILE. (*See* ARCADY LIBRARY).

Lucas (Winifred).

UNITS: Poems. Fcap. 8vo. 3s. 6d. net.

Lynch (Hannah).

THE GREAT GALEOTO AND FOLLY OR SAINTLINESS. Two Plays, from the Spanish of JOSÉ ECHEGARAY, with an Introduction. Small 4to. 5s 6d. net.

Marzials (Theo.).

THE GALLERY OF PIGEONS AND OTHER POEMS. Post 8vo. 4s. 6d. net. [*Transferred to the present Publisher.*

The Mayfair Set.

Each volume fcap. 8vo. 3s. 6d. net.

I. THE AUTOBIOGRAPHY OF A BOY. Passages selected by his friend G. S. STREET. With a Title-page designed by C. W. FURSE. [*Fifth Edition.*

II. THE JONESES AND THE ASTERISKS. A Story in Monologue. By GERALD CAMPBELL. With a Title-page and 6 Illustrations by F. H. TOWNSEND. [*Second Edition.*

The Mayfair Set—continued.

III. SELECT CONVERSATIONS WITH AN UNCLE, NOW EXTINCT. By H. G. WELLS. With a Title-page by F. H. TOWNSEND.

IV. FOR PLAIN WOMEN ONLY. By GEORGE FLEMING. With a Title-page by PATTEN WILSON.

V. THE FEASTS OF AUTOLYCUS: THE DIARY OF A GREEDY WOMAN. Edited by ELIZABETH ROBINS PENNELL. With a Title-page by PATTEN WILSON.

VI. MRS. ALBERT GRUNDY: OBSERVATIONS IN PHILISTIA. By HAROLD FREDERIC. With a Title-page by PATTEN WILSON. [Second Edition.

Meredith (George).

THE FIRST PUBLISHED PORTRAIT OF THIS AUTHOR, engraved on the wood by W. BISCOMBE GARDNER, after the painting by G. F. WATTS. Proof copies on Japanese vellum, signed by painter and engraver. £1 1s. net.

Meynell (Mrs.).

POEMS. Fcap. 8vo. 3s. 6d. net. [Fifth Edition.

THE RHYTHM OF LIFE AND OTHER ESSAYS. Fcap. 8vo. 3s. 6d. net. [Fifth Edition.

THE COLOUR OF LIFE AND OTHER ESSAYS. Fcap 8vo. 3s. 6d. net. [Fifth Edition.

THE CHILDREN. Fcap. 8vo. 3s. 6d. net. [Second Edition.

Miller (Joaquin).

THE BUILDING OF THE CITY BEAUTIFUL. Fcap. 8vo. With a Decorated Cover. 5s. net.

Money-Coutts (F. B.).

POEMS. With Title-page designed by PATTEN WILSON. Crown 8vo. 3s. 6d. net.

Monkhouse (Allan).

BOOKS AND PLAYS: A Volume of Essays on Meredith, Borrow, Ibsen, and others. Crown 8vo. 5s. net.

A DELIVERANCE. (See KEYNOTES SERIES.)

Nesbit (E.).

A POMANDER OF VERSE. With a Title-page and Cover designed by LAURENCE HOUSMAN. Crown 8vo. 5s. net.

IN HOMESPUN. (See KEYNOTES SERIES.)

Nettleship (J. T.).

ROBERT BROWNING: Essays and Thoughts. Crown 8vo. 5s. 6d. net. [Third Edition.

Noble (Jas. Ashcroft).

THE SONNET IN ENGLAND AND OTHER ESSAYS. Title-page and Cover Design by AUSTIN YOUNG. Crown 8vo. 5s. net.

Also 50 copies large paper 12s. 6d. net

Oppenheim (Michael).

A HISTORY OF THE ADMINISTRATION OF THE ROYAL NAVY, and of Merchant Shipping in relation to the Navy from MDIX to MDCLX, with an introduction treating of the earlier period. With Illustrations. Demy 8vo. 15s. net.

O'Shaughnessy (Arthur).

HIS LIFE AND HIS WORK. With Selections from his Poems. By LOUISE CHANDLER MOULTON. Portrait and Cover Design. Fcap. 8vo. 5s. net.

Oxford Characters.

A series of lithographed portraits by WILL ROTHENSTEIN, with text by F. YORK POWELL and others. 200 copies only, folio, buckram. £3 3s. net.

25 special large paper copies containing proof impressions of the portraits signed by the artist, £6 6s. net.

Peters (Wm. Theodore).

POSIES OUT OF RINGS. With Title-page by PATTEN WILSON. Sq. 16mo. 2s. 6d. net.

Pierrot's Library.

Each volume with Title-page, Cover and End Papers, designed by AUBREY BEARDSLEY. Sq. 16mo. 2s. net.

I. PIERROT. By H. DE VERE STACPOOLE.
II. MY LITTLE LADY ANNE. By Mrs. EGERTON CASTLE.
III. SIMPLICITY. By A. T. G. PRICE.
IV. MY BROTHER. By VINCENT BROWN.

The following are in preparation:

V. DEATH, THE KNIGHT, AND THE LADY. By H. DE VERE STACPOOLE.
VI. MR. PASSINGHAM. By THOMAS COBB.
VII. TWO IN CAPTIVITY. By VINCENT BROWN.

Plarr (Victor).

IN THE DORIAN MOOD: Poems. With Title-page by PATTEN WILSON. Crown 8vo. 5s. net.

Posters in Miniature: over

250 reproductions of French, English and American Posters with Introduction by EDWARD PENFIELD. Large crown 8vo. 5s. net.

Radford (Dollie).

SONGS AND OTHER VERSES. With a Title-page by PATTEN WILSON. Fcap. 8vo. 4s. 6d. net.

Rhys (Ernest).

A LONDON ROSE AND OTHER RHYMES. With Title-page designed by SELWYN IMAGE. Crown 8vo. 5s. net.

Robertson (John M.).

ESSAYS TOWARDS A CRITICAL METHOD. (New Series.) Crown 8vo. 5s. net. [*In preparation.*

St. Cyres (Lord).

THE LITTLE FLOWERS OF ST. FRANCIS: A new rendering into English of the Fioretti di San Francesco. Crown 8vo. 5s. net. [*In preparation.*

Seaman (Owen).

THE BATTLE OF THE BAYS. Fcap. 8vo. 3s. 6d. net.

Sedgwick (Jane Minot).

SONGS FROM THE GREEK. Fcap. 8vo. 3s. 6d. net.

Setoun (Gabriel).

THE CHILD WORLD: Poems. With over 200 Illustrations by CHARLES ROBINSON. Crown 8vo, gilt edges or uncut. 5s. net.

Sharp (Evelyn).

WYMPS: Fairy Tales. With Coloured Illustrations by MABEL DEARMER. Small 4to, decorated cover. 4s. 6d. net.

AT THE RELTON ARMS. (*See* KEYNOTES SERIES.)

THE MAKING OF A PRIG. (*See* FOUR-AND-SIXPENNY NOVELS.)

Shore (Louisa).

POEMS. With an appreciation by FREDERIC HARRISON and a Portrait. Fcap. 8vo. 5s. net.

Short Stories Series.

Each volume Post 8vo. Coloured edges. 2s. 6d. net.

I. SOME WHIMS OF FATE. By MÉNIE MURIEL DOWIE.
II. THE SENTIMENTAL VIKINGS. By R. V. RISLEY.
III. SHADOWS OF LIFE. By Mrs. MURRAY HICKSON.

Stevenson (Robert Louis).

PRINCE OTTO. A Rendering in French by EGERTON CASTLE. With Frontispiece, Title-page, and Cover Design by D. Y. CAMERON. Crown 8vo. 7s. 6d. net.

Also 50 copies on large paper, uniform in size with the Edinburgh Edition of the Works.

A CHILD'S GARDEN OF VERSES. With over 150 Illustrations by CHARLES ROBINSON. Crown 8vo. 5s. net. [*Second Edition.*

Stimson (F. J.)

KING NOANETT. A Romance of Devonshire Settlers in New England. Illustrated. Large crown 8vo. 5s. net.

Stoddart (Thos. Tod).

THE DEATH WAKE. With an Introduction by ANDREW LANG. Fcap. 8vo. 5s. net.

Street (G. S.).

EPISODES. Post 8vo. 3s. net.

MINIATURES AND MOODS. Fcap. 8vo. 3s. net. [*Both transferred to the present Publisher.*

QUALES EGO: A FEW REMARKS, IN PARTICULAR AND AT LARGE. Fcap. 8vo. 3s. 6d. net.

THE AUTOBIOGRAPHY OF A BOY. (*See* MAYFAIR SET.)

THE WISE AND THE WAYWARD. (*See* FOUR - AND - SIXPENNY NOVELS.)

Swettenham (F. A.)

MALAY SKETCHES. With a Title-page and Cover Design by PATTEN WILSON. Crown 8vo. 5s. net.
[*Second Edition.*

Tabb (John B.).

POEMS. Sq. 32mo. 4s. 6d. net.

Tennyson (Frederick).

POEMS OF THE DAY AND YEAR. With a Title-page designed by PATTEN WILSON. Crown 8vo. 5s. net.

Thimm (Carl A.).

A COMPLETE BIBLIOGRAPHY OF FENCING AND DUELLING, AS PRACTISED BY ALL EUROPEAN NATIONS FROM THE MIDDLE AGES TO THE PRESENT DAY. With a Classified Index, arranged Chronologically according to Languages. Illustrated with numerous Portraits of Ancient and Modern Masters of the Art. Title-pages and Frontispieces of some of the earliest works. Portrait of the Author by WILSON STEER, and Title page designed by PATTEN WILSON. 4to. 21s. net.

Thompson (Francis)

POEMS. With Frontispiece, Title-page, and Cover Design by LAURENCE HOUSMAN. Pott 4to. 5s. net. [*Fourth Edition.*

SISTER-SONGS: An Offering to Two Sisters. With Frontispiece, Title-page, and Cover Design by LAURENCE HOUSMAN. Pott 4to. 5s. net.

Thoreau (Henry David).

POEMS OF NATURE. Selected and edited by HENRY S. SALT and FRANK B. SANBORN, with a Title-page designed by PATTEN WILSON. Fcap. 8vo. 4s. 6d. net.

Traill (H. D.).

THE BARBAROUS BRITISHERS: A Tip-top Novel. With Title and Cover Design by AUBREY BEARDSLEY. Crown 8vo, wrapper. 1s. net.

FROM CAIRO TO THE SOUDAN FRONTIER. With Cover Design by PATTEN WILSON. Crown 8vo. 5s. net.

Tynan Hinkson (Katharine)

CUCKOO SONGS. With Title-page and Cover Design by LAURENCE HOUSMAN. Fcap. 8vo. 5s. 1 et.

MIRACLE PLAYS. OUR LORD'S COMING AND CHILDHOOD. With 6 Illustrations, Title-page, and Cover Design by PATTEN WILSON. Fcap. 8vo. 4s. 6d. net.

Walton and Cotton.

THE COMPLEAT ANGLER. Edited by RICHARD LE GALLIENNE. Illustrated by EDMUND H. NEW. Fcap. 4to, decorated cover. 15s. net.

Also to be had in thirteen 1s. parts.

Watson (Rosamund Marriott).

VESPERTILIA AND OTHER POEMS. With a Title-page designed by R. ANNING BELL. Fcap. 8vo. 4s. 6d. net.

A SUMMER NIGHT AND OTHER POEMS. New Edition. With a Decorative Title-page. Fcap. 8vo. 3s. net.

Watson (William).

THE FATHER OF THE FOREST AND OTHER POEMS. With New Photogravure Portrait of the Author Fcap. 8vo, buckram. 3s. 6d. net.
[*Fifth Edition.*

ODES AND OTHER POEMS. Fcap 8vo, buckram. 4s. 6d. net.
[*Fourth Edition.*

Watson (William)—*continued.*

THE ELOPING ANGELS: A Caprice Square 16mo, buckram. 3s. 6d. net.   [*Second Edition.*

EXCURSIONS IN CRITICISM : being some Prose Recreations of a Rhymer. Crown 8vo, buckram. 5s. net.   [*Second Edition.*

THE PRINCE'S QUEST AND OTHER POEMS. With a Bibliographical Note added. Fcap. 8vo, buckram. 4s. 6d. net.   [*Third Edition.*

THE PURPLE EAST : A Series of Sonnets on England's Desertion of Armenia. With a Frontispiece after G. F. WATTS, R.A. Fcap. 8vo, wrappers. 1s. net.
      [*Third Edition.*

THE YEAR OF SHAME. With an Introduction by the BISHOP OF HEREFORD. Fcap. 8vo. 2s. 6d. net.   [*Second Edition.*

Watt (Francis).

THE LAW'S LUMBER ROOM. Fcap. 8vo. 3s. 6d. net.
      [*Second Edition.*

Watts-Dunton (Theodore).

POEMS. Crown 8vo. 5s. net.
      [*In preparation.*

There will also be an *Edition de Luxe* of this volume printed at the Kelmscott Press.

Wenzell (A. B.)

IN VANITY FAIR. 70 Drawings. Oblong folio. 15s. net.

Wharton (H. T.)

SAPPHO. Memoir, Text, Selected Renderings, and a Literal Translation by HENRY THORNTON WHARTON. With 3 Illustrations in Photogravure, and a Cover designed by AUBREY BEARDSLEY. Fcap. 8vo. 7s. 6d. net.   [*Third Edition.*

THE YELLOW BOOK

An Illustrated Quarterly.

Pott 4to. 5s. net.